Elmer is not what you would call
the garden spot of the small worlds.

If you are to gain a correct impression of how we operate, and how the MerryThought works, you might logically begin with the observation that all of us on Woo possess the same name: Mary Carnivorous Rabbit.

Ideas, someone said, are dime a dozen—unless you don't have one. Was it Eulalia?

It all started when one of us, I forget which one, suggested we banish all hereditary titles and declare a Radical Republic.

They lied to me about the reality of things here on Muazzez. About the foundation of these, their basis, their fundament, the profound bottom of things.

Fern would not have known how to say it without my help; Fern was slow, and I, her beloved, was fast.

Because I was a very tall young girl, every time I would walk along the Charcoal Road a group of short and brutish boys would pelt me with stones. I say "because" but I really do not know.

Linda Susan is a small, bright world.

Author's Note;

All of the worlds described herein are real, though none of them are on any map. Any atlas of what are known as asteroids or planetoids will list them all. The prophecy of Eulalia referred to throughout this volume, is simply the notion that all these strange, miniature worlds were originally part of one, larger, and presumably happier place.

OTHER BOOKS BY MAC WELLMAN

PLAYS – COLLECTIONS

The Bad Infinity
Cellophane
Crowtet 1
Crowtet 2
The Land Beyond the Forest

INDIVIDUAL PLAYS

Bad Penny
Harm's Way
The Professional Frenchman
Sincerity Forever
Infrared

POETRY

Satires
A Shelf in Woop's Clothing
Miniature
Strange Elegies

NOVELS

The Fortuneteller: A Jest
Annie Salem: An American Tale
Q's Q: An Arboreal Narrative

About the Author

Mac Wellman's recent work includes a play, *Two September*, an opera (with David Lang), *The Difficulty of Crossing a Field*, and a novel, *Q's Q*.

In 2003, Mac Wellman received his third Obie, for Lifetime Achievement. In 2004, he received an award from the Foundaion for Contemporary Art.

Mac Wellman is Professor of Play Writing at Brooklyn College.

A CHRONICLE OF THE
MADNESS OF SMALL WORLDS

By
Mac Wellman

Special Thanks: The Corporation of Yaddo, the MacDowell Colony, and the Bellagio Study and Conference Center of the Rockefeller Foundation.

The names, characters, events and asteroids portrayed in these stories are either the product of the author's imagination or are used fictitiously. Any resemblance to actual persons, living or dead, or to real events and asteroids is entirely coincidental.

Printed on acid-free paper — Printed in the United States of America

Several of the stories have been previously published in slightly different form in the following magazines and anthologies: "Elmer" in *Noir Mechanics* (1993), "Linda Susan" in *Theater* (1995), "Wu World Woo" in *2000andWhat?* (1996), "Muazzez" in *Here Lies* (2001), and "1965UU" in *Mantis* (2003).

ISBN 978-0-9639192-6-7

First Edition. 2008

Cover and Book Design by Beverly Garrity

Cover Painting by Karl Roeseler

Printing by McNaughton & Gunn

Trip Street Press books are distributed by
Small Press Distribution
1341 Seventh Street, Berkeley, CA 94710
www.spdbooks.org
800.869.7553 or 510.524.1668

Trip Street Press | P. O. Box 190201 | San Francisco, CA 94119

A CHRONICLE OF THE
MADNESS OF SMALL WORLDS

toc

table of contents

!?:

{The Hats of Elmer}

Elmer is not what you would call the garden spot of the small worlds. On the surface of it there is nothing to distinguish from a score of other, similarly shaped, eccentric, grim, little planetoids. But Elmer always feels different—crummier, less classy, more deadend and hopeless. The air, what there is of it, contained the barest suggestion of spoiled food—of the ripe remains of box lunches left over from a picnic at a far ago county fair. But of course there has never been a county fair on Elmer. Elmer is the kind of place where folks go when they've given up all hope of finding a meaning to the empty riddle of their old lives, or an opening to any new one. The locals mostly stand around in little venomous knots gossiping and scheming. Frankly, it just as easy to make someone's life a living hell by gossip as by physical abuse. This incidentally involves much less hard, physical labor, and since the locals are, on the whole, an indolent bunch, the course of Elmerish society creeps along the slow, safe predictable low road of slander and character assassination.

1

One of my childhood acquaintances, Monsoor X, ended up after a scandalous bit of flapdoodle at the Corn Bank, as a minor official on Elmer. X had been something of a celebrity on Linda

Susan, but then Linda Susan is the kind of place that stimulates thoughts of a boundless future, heroic acts, wishes-come-true and the standard poppycock associated with a blue sky, abundant hydrocarbons and a more or less consistent orbital eccentricity. Ah, but the golden skies of Linda Susan and the soft winning-ways of her inhabitants are a light-year of country-miles removed—in terms of grace, civility and hedonistic overplus—from the nasty hubbub, the stupid and empty sham of social relations on Elmer.

Most citizens of Elmer, for instance, wear the traditional boxy hat, generally made of cardboard or sheet-rock, and shoddily decorated with bright-colored baubles, thumbtacks, old postcards, trinkets (such as those used by the merchants of the Olden Times in barter on various of the smaller worlds); but on Elmer these hats—grotesque, unsightly affairs—useless at best (for there is no "weather" to speak of on Elmer), serve only as a provocation. For even the locals find them stupid and uncouth. So the wearing of hats, on Elmer at least, has only a theoretical relation to either pleasure, utility, or the reaffirmation of the social bond. Indeed, the wearing of hats on Elmer constitutes but one more in a series of more or less intentional and more or less hostile acts which have led to the common characterization, as mentioned above: Elmer is the world of deadends, anomie, an existential cul de sac.

Our entire civilization amounts to a provocation—a bitter taunt. Now, my friend Monsieur X had in mind to change all this. Being a true child of Linda Susan, X was an incurable optimist, not to mention an ambidextrous son-of-a-gun—and prehensile in the tail department. X was from the dark side of Linda Susan, a region of fine, azure sand (the final decay product of an antediluvian nuclear dump from aeons past?), and a few hollowed-out and petrified chimneys of archaic anthill; these gave a fine perch from which wide-angle perspectives of the world might be surveyed. X surmised the relatively untouched dark side of Elmer might be worth converting into a similarly, fabulously attractive place. This was not a totally mad idea, for the dark side of Elmer was covered with a fine, granular soot-like substance of unknown composition; and on bright nights, particularly during periods of occultation of the sun or close encounters with Elmer-passing coeval worlds, the dells and downs of the dark side would give off a ghostly, semi-iridescent glitter so that the whole supple shape of its hills, crevasses, buttes and arroyos would seem the sensuous body of some immense but inexpressibly sensitive living being. X thought the place suggested something of the slowly gathering ardor of the female climax; the inhabitants of Elmer had a more crass interpretation, but of that later. X had the idea to organize a Festival of the Dark Side, which would celebrate the beauties of the Elmerish dunes in a variety of exciting ways. Hotels for tourists would be built. A monorail system erected on the stony ridges surrounding the main expanse of the darkest regions would thereby provide a spectacular panorama for the visitors. But X was native to the most peaceful of places, Linda Susan, and therefore could not imagine the passions native to Elmer, especially since these were, in the main, merely pointless and obstructive—indeed, their workings out in the pathways of Elmerish chronology had never benefitted a single soul. But that did not prevent them from occupying a central position in the psychic weather of the place. A special facet of many of the small worlds that should be noted here is an unusual blending into the physical entity of the world itself, of the spiritual and psychic character of the place. This happens too on larger worlds, but normally takes centuries for its effect to become perceptible. On smaller worlds like Elmer the interpenetration of the two orders of being is startling, complex and evident to all who are capable of noticing detail at all. Alas, sunny-dispositioned X was not among these unfortunately, and he paid the price for his incurable solar optimism (or rather his investors did). Anyone with an eye half-open would've been skeptical about such a project, such a happy Linda Susanish pipe-dream as this, ever succeeding in a craven, woebegone sinkhole like Elmer right from the start. And there was a further complication that began to be noticed a little later than the first, most obvious disaster; a complication that begins to loom far more frightening than any mere mercantile collapse. But I am getting ahead of myself,

3

and I am doing so because X was a close, personal friend of mine, and I am not looking forward to telling the story of his folly. X, of course, was not X's true name; to reveal this would be to add unnecessary opprobrium to a fine old family, friends of my kinfolk.

So I did warn X, having had an inkling that something might turn unfathomably awry. All you had to do was stand athwart any of the saloons, or coffee shoppes, or card parlors, in any of the tin-roofed ramshackle towns of Elmer and listen to the buzz, the low hum of poisonous talk, the wicked murmuratio of the hollow-faced, insolent, staring faces, and you would know there was trouble brewing. But even I, who suspected the worst, could not for the life of me identify the precise root core of the rumor, nor who had started it, nor when, nor what its true message might be, nor whether it possessed a purpose, a plan or intent. So, I may be forgiven for not sticking to my guns when I confronted X on the subject just before the gala grand opening of the hotel of the Sacred Crow (the crow is the totem animal of Elmer), complete with a brigade of brightly dressed regimental stand-ins of no particular world, or no particular army; hot air balloons with upbeat messages and vivid commercial logos emblazoned on them; folkloric performers in native costume (though none, sadly, native to dour Elmer). For as the haze of aerosol and particle debris kicked up by the bowling matches, horse races, Indian-club throwing competitions and the general hubbub of celebration cleared, a strange and gloomy sight presented itself. A huge a mountain of crazy Elmerish hats. Hats thrown down as a provocation by those left out of the festivities, immigrants apparently, from remote regions of the bright side, all the way around Elmer. Now individual Elmerish hats are quite enough to repel the sensibilities of most civilized persons and to arouse antisocial feelings, not to mention symptoms of nausea, wretchedness and vomitation among the susceptible; so you can imagine the effect of a whole mountain of these. Somehow, the effect was more than simply additive; it grew repulsively exponential. This jiggling, horrid heap of trashy, lowclass, barbaric, unsightly hats of Elmer conveyed such a taste of gross

4

unwelcome that, on the spot, all merriment ceased and the crowds of visitors stood around in small groups, embarrassed, abashed, ashamed, all feeling taken advantage of, had. My friend X leapt about, up and down, trying to restore the spirit of good feeling and festivity and so forth he had so enthusiastically nurtured; but to no avail. The grand opening had transformed willy-nilly into a complete bust, an entrepreneurial dry hole.

Finally, from across a wide, wind-swept dry lake bed, a low roar went up, like the cry of a beast in pain or a state of fear, or that of a stupid but powerful animal who thinks such an outburst will scare off rivals for his meat and his mate. We squinted and covered our eyes, and finally could make out a vast crowd of Elmervians, who had assembled there, in mockery of us. The consequences of Monsieur X's folly were, thus, quick and harsh: he was tarred and feathered and ridden out of town on a rail. Of course, on Elmer, the only feathers available are crow's feather, which are black obviously; while the tar on that world is a thick, unwholesome white (like some nightmare cream, or a soft cheese). As a result,there was a reverse-field doubling of his shame. Poor Monsieur X, he whose only flaw was the misplaced desire to give pleasure, was not heard from again, even on Elmer; though there are those who claim to have come across him, on various worlds, in different disguises, with different clothes, speaking different languages, sporting different aliases, in different contexts, altogether a different man— although still the same man—haunted forever by the specter of his Elmerish shame.

▬ ▬ {*The Madness of Small Worlds*}

The more serious consequences of Monsoor X's escapade, which I have alluded to, was wholly inadvertent and inescapable. Indeed, if you were to hang a plaque with motto below a picture of Elmer, glumly suspended like a Scotch Egg in the murky ruins of outer space, I have no doubt that plaque would bear the legend: *Inadvertent and Inescapable*. For Monsoor X brought with him, inadvertently, as did those of his clients hailing also from Linda Susan, small quantities of the famed azure dust of that world. And this beautiful, blue dust—and the sparkling, black soot of Elmer, when brought together in close, mineral proximity, reacted in a strange, indeed, in an almost incomprehensible fashion: the two dusts wiggled and foamed. They popped and hissed and gurgled and growled and boiled up with Elmerish bad temper. Then—after some days of this chemico-choleric behavior—quasi-human shapes, anachronistically called "sandmen" would rise up, out of this primordial mess, coughing and belching, swaging and scrambling about, making a general nuisance of themselves. Now of course these eerie shapes only appear human, for it is impossible for them to be human. However, the sandmen's strange behavior seemed to be a parody of the human, for they would reply to any challenge or salute by throwing the challenge or salute back upon the person who had issued it, but with an insulting, slightly hostile and definitely tactless hauteur. When struck or attacked with weapons they would simply collapse and literally fall apart, leaving an oily, pestiferous ash. Certain persons quickly became obsessed with this ash, and would rub it on their faces, limbs and bellies. Some who actually ingested the material, like snuff, or swallowed small servings of it or mixed yet smaller portions with tea or mineral water, soon began to suffer the fearful effects of an unspeakable poisoning; or—in a few ghastly and incredible cases—actually began to transform into pseudo-sandmen themselves, though all of these died before the sickening micro-mineralization of their bodies became complete. Some of these spent the torment of their final hours making a strange series of little calls or yelps, as if attempting to speak in an unknown tongue, or pronounce the unsayable word; perhaps a garbled version of the name of some loved one, or the hidden name of the poison itself, or whatever phantasm sickness had conjured in the dissolution of consciousness. For all seemed to be engaged—while in the throes of death itself—in a powerful, spiritual agon. An agon empty of meaning, an agon of nothing reared upon nowhere. This cruelest phase of the plague was quickly over, however; for soon people had learned how to handle the peculiar substance with appropriate caution; moreover, all of the sandmen came to be destroyed, and all the ash of their fugitive remains scattered, sealed up in metal drums and buried, with care taken that no mixing of two sands, that of Elmer and that of Linda Susan, ever occur again. But the trouble with small collisions of fine dust, like the products of the human mind, is that no man can say where they go, or where they are, or what harm they may do, after they have once been set into motion, however creaky or crabwise. For a large number of us, both the Elmerish and Linda Susans—not to mention a few like myself—peripatetic accidentals, wandering doctors of no doctrine, the unlucky, in short all those who had been even microscopically contaminated, began, in the intervening weeks and months, to notice symptoms of the malady soon to be described as "the madness of small worlds". Those of us who are aware we are subject to its fits, palsy, its visionary dementia, often are better prepared than those poor innocents, mere digits of the general unenlightenment, who imagine themselves immune to its ravages. We who are certified victims of the Madness must carry a mark identifying us as what we are. The mark itself is called a "murder". Often we do not like this rule, since our perilous identity is a thing we are proud of—many times the Madness renders us far more socially successful, intriguing, and in a strange sense—and as individuals even, individually considered—*unique*. We derive pleasure from this uniqueness, or at least I do; although it is an established fact that most sufferers of the Madness of Small Worlds are tedious, verbose, intellectual frauds and spiritual incontinents who are about as amusing as a... talking crow.

For I am convinced by what I have seen of life since the beginnings of the Great Infection that, whereas all the others similarly affected have become sleazy, derelict, emotional cripples and sociopathic parasites, *I* have realized my higher nature and—thanks to the ironic fates who rule the dark ways of the

7

malady—have become a vessel of the hidden spirit world, a communicating chamber, if you will, between and amongst the myriad, interconnected small worlds and ghost worlds, as they impinge through time, myth, destiny and bulldiddly on the unknowing lives of those to come. And those to come whose passing has already been written in the big book of Tlooth. But all of us who are carriers harbor the deep conviction that the most virulent cases, as I have already indicated are the undiagnosed; these are our brethren who cannot imagine such a thing, so great is their fear of us, of hearing the softly whispered vocables of our secret creed, of joining our sudden fits of joy and dancing, of coming to grips with our frequent bouts of torpor and depression, of dreaming with us of the crossroads where time toggles act, and act toggles thought, and thought toggles love, and love toggles death, and death toggles time. Of touching our sensual lips and wings with their puritanical hooks and fins. Of seeing that we are them, only unveiled and brighter.

More of the nature of the malady it would be pointless to outline at this point, and pointedly so, since none of us inhabitants of the small worlds is any good at all at what you would call theory. That enterprise went belly-up millennia ago when the mother of all worlds went critical and blew. Hence, you will find no macro-cosmologists or deconstructionists among us, and if our hats are not as diabolically odd and off-putting as the hats of Elmer, they are still cut from strange cloth, and would cause a gasp of shock from the mouth of any but the most robust theoretician. And he who does not construe the wider implications of this fact walks, as it were, barefoot on broken glass, when he goes among us beneath the rat-colored, moonless nights of Elmer.

━ ━ ━ *{On the Difference Between Smooth & Woolly}*

Enough of my troubles though; let's get down to business. The picture I have painted of Elmer is, I know, not a pretty one. This is perhaps unfair, for it is recorded variously that Elmer was at one time considered quite a remarkable place, right up there with Wild, Wolfiana, and Tuulikki, as a potentially fabulous garden spa. But that was before philosophers had distinguished between Smooth and Woolly Worlds, much to the disadvantage of the latter. The evident need, amazing as it may seem, simply had not occurred to people then, even to the supposedly wise and learned, the Elders of the Academy of [!?:] and the Priests of Tlooth. Clearly, the ways of prehistoric humanity do not reveal their secrets with ease, even under the scrutiny of contemporary analytical tools, statistics, the dice, and the scissors. But once the fatal judgment—with respect to primal woolliness, that is—had been made, things rapidly fell apart on Elmer, and all the fine hopes, for tourism, for development, of real estate and industry alike, quickly vanished. A Small World Certificate of Woolliness usually always means the kiss of death as far as investment capital is concerned. This may seem unfair, and a bit like the proverbial self-fulfilling prophecy; but it is nevertheless a fact of life on many of the small worlds. The fact that the issue of innate, primal woolliness can nowadays only be accurately determined with the most sophisticated of modern instruments does not help matters, since the common lot of most small worlds have established rituals and customs for divining the answer to this question so that they often reject the findings of the official staff from the Board of Certification. This has led to scuffles, shouting and shoving matches, vandalism, and, on a few occasions, wholesale rioting, massacre, and, in one instance at least, civil war. It is a shame that no one has been able to calm the fears of the big investors, whose interest in the whole diadem of Small Worlds has been falling off most precipitously in recent decades anyway. But these power-   ━ 9
ful men are obviously fixed in their ways and no amount of arguing will convince them that a woolly world is as stable as a smooth one. This prejudice must date from a very ancient time,

and so has become almost a reflex on the part of the big banks, investment houses, and other institutions of high finance.

When I was younger I used to go for long camping trips to the remote, mountainous regions of equatorial Elmer—the Mountains of Fear lay there. I would scurry up and down the tumult of crags, peaks, circs and sheer rock faces. This activity was both strenuous and dangerous, but that never bothered me. I was young, full of energy and never paid any attention to the warnings of my elders. Time and time again my friends would inquire of me, my aunts and uncles would beg to find out, what was the fascination for me of this strange place? I would laugh at this, and come out with all the standard cliches: I wanted to prove myself, how exercise toughens the body and clears the mind, how my sensitive inner self required solitude among the sublime masterworks of nature. All the usual jazz. Guff, all of it. For, in truth, none of this had any bearing on my hunger for hikes and trail-blazing adventure among the jagged peaks of the Mountains of Fear; it was that I possessed an unquenchable and wholly inexplicable desire to follow the wiggly lines of bright marble and mica schist, and the dark bands of basalt and slate, and the archaic formations of which they were part as they crept up and down individual summits, for I imagined this strange graphology contained things I ought to know. Indeed, the squiggles, marks, bands, stripes and complex fractures mimicked a vocabulary of symbols I knew were so crucial to the culture of a people, any people. But the fascination I felt and have never been able fully to explain has something to do with the more basic question of what a thing is, when it is physically bent, twisted, folded, burned and smashed, made molten and poured into a pattern, or dropped from a high place to splat on a hard surface; or the way materials break and splinter, and radiate out, to be percolated through other structures, or embedded there, often after being deposited by a violent explosion nearby. So for as long as I could remember, the world I knew as Elmer, was a wiggly, asymmetrical, wild-hearted, wickedly irregular, non-linear sort of place: it was woolly. The smooth parts—and there were only a few of these, dry lake beds, places where a glacier has sheared stone across a flat vector—these were deceptive, the ironic fibs of nature. The true Elmer was complex, complex, multiform, and thoroughly woolly; and, as I was an inhabitant of a world ineradicably woolly, I too participated in that woolliness. So the stigma of the Certification had no effect on me, really. Although I could see it caused deep unease all around me, real pain and metaphysical self-doubt. My wild tramps in forbidden places like the Mountains of Fear, corny as it may seem, hardened me and made me wiser, stronger and more able to deal with the crazy multiplex non-conformity I have seen all around me on Elmer, even in the State House, the shopping centers, and in the beer halls and gambling parlors of the bright side. For when I became puzzled by the strange mindset of those not like me, those whose entire life seemed violence incarnate, senseless, aberrant or mad, I could pull back my social antennae for a moment and focus on the beautiful squiggle of human eccentricity that could be observed, independent of personal identity and social matrix (or one's stake in the matter, for that matter), wiggling and worming their way, this way and that, through the hard, tightly-packed human social-matter of the room. The rhythm of this wiggling and worming, though utterly devoid of meaning in any conventional sense, either in Elmerish or any other terms, took on a significance all its own, as though it were like the deep, embedded layering of the formation of the Fear Range. This rhythm was a deep structure to be sure, but a wholly, open-ended, and therefore useless. That is why Linda Susanish beach bungalows don't look right on Elmer. That is why there are so few churches on Elmer; why there is no influx of venture capital; why no one has any interest in the doings of Big Tom Tomorrow here; why the vampires have all fled to the neo-gothic romantic ruins of Hedwerthia rather lap up the rich, but woolly Elmerish blood. That is why not a shred of respect adheres to any of the fables common to many of the surrounding worlds, fables   11 which have long been forgotten here. That is why Gump left his shoes here, and the Standing Monument of Broom fell over, much to the amusement of the local shepherds, who make fun of the spot, and will shear only their black sheep on the ruined plinth; it is why they piss upon the other stones, and gleefully curse the day they were born. This is why the people of Elmer wear such unusual hats, such wiggly and woolly hats.

━━ ━━ ━━ ━━ *{The Great Din}*

Ah, but the strangest fact about the world of Elmer is something that does not even exist in the language of Elmer. (Isn't the strangest fact about a world always something which does not exist in its language?) This phenomenon was first noticed at least 14 certainties ago by the humble priest, Jesus Unusual Cauliflower, who once upon a time made a complaint to his fellow agriculturists (Jesus Unusual Cauliflower was a common laborer in a commune dedicated to the harvesting of certain mystic herbs in the uplands of Nope Lock). At the start he complained of headaches, and as these were of the unusual variety and did not respond to the normal medicines, Jesus Unusual Cauliflower sought spiritual guidance. Alas, the elders of the commune were unable to detect any spiritual malady that might explain the headaches. Forbearance, they advised. This is your cross to bear, Brother Jesus.

But soon the headaches changed ever so slowly into a dim sensation of sound, a deep mechanical clangor. At first Brother Jesus could not identify the source of this sound, because as far as he could tell it came from all directions at once. A definite semi-regular, quasi-rhythmical banging and clangor, a booming and striking, a ringing and gonging. But soon Brother Jesus realized it was the body of Elmer itself that was the source of the noises, and that these were increasing day by day. At first the others, including the elders, smiled and dismissed the idea as the sad result of Jesus Unusual Cauliflower's condition, but then one day someone else heard the sound. Then another, and another. Someone who was good at names dubbed it the Great Din, and as the noise level rose around everyone like an invisible box of four invisible walls, all the inhabitants of Elmer prayed for release, for the sound grew steadily worse, and began as time went on to become not merely an annoyance, but a positive torment, a pain.

People would lose their ability to deal with it, and go mad. The Din could penetrate the thickest of walls, the tightest closed door and window; even earplugs only slightly reduced the immense tremendum. Cults of the maddened sprang up in various places to celebrate the Din and its power, the justice and wisdom and splendor of the Din. Victims were exposed with unplugged ears on the Temple of Woofer and Tweeter, who became the Gog and Magog of the new order. Strange dances could be observed at all times, in the oddest of places, to placate the Din. Law and order ceased entirely for a time as the noise threatened to put an end to all the arts and sciences, to all farming, food gathering, and industry. Life became a sheer unremitting horror, as more and more people went mad and leapt from high places into the empty seabeds of Elmer. Truly, the end was nigh.

Abruptly, people noticed the noise begin to fade. This happened very quickly, and for no apparent reason. Indeed, after only a week all the complex architecture, the maddening structure of timbre and cross-rhythm and rumble had thinned out to a distant, wavering hum. A bothersome bumblebee buzz. The deep pulsations of the lowest registers could of course still be felt, but not heard.

One day the Din was no more and people responded by silently gathering in public places, parks and amphitheaters, in traffic islands and cemeteries. Scribes of the Legislative Assembly prepared a document ordering a round of cheers, a series of choral chants of public acclamation. All the citizenry, and I must confess I was among that happy crowd on that momen- ▬ 13
tous occasion, inhaled deeply and with a fullness of heart that one could never imagine in the relatively soft, permissive times we live in now.

We opened our mouths as one, and as one cried out:

 [1]

There was a silence as deep and as fathomless as the Din before it. Jesus Unusual Cauliflower, who by now was an old, twisted relic of a man, got down on his knees and wept. We could not hear his cries any more than our own before them; we were all deaf, totally deaf. The silence has claimed us as surely as the Din, and we know this time there will be no respite. The thrall of the Din is absolute, incommensurable and beyond knowing, willing or belief. It has become the weather of our lives, our condition, and the medium through which our very being is expressed. We have been in a state of awe ever since, but because the silence is a condition we all share, it does not divide us. But certainly it does mark us off against aliens of all sorts and the other worldy: those whose ears still respond to the world's meaningless jangle. We despise this jangle, and consider ourselves superior to all others. Perhaps the Din itself ended when we became enlightened, deaf in the words of those still bamboozled, those like you who read this, but read without understanding. Perhaps the din and the silence are one, who can say? Indeed, there are two opposing congregations of our major church, congregations based on diametrical interpretations of this mystery. Whatever else, our elders are always very careful to inspect closely anyone, even among those suffering the Madness, who complains of an unusual headache.

[1] A picture of the noise no one hears

━ ━ ━ ━ ━ [Who I Really Am]

Did I tell you that I am a big fellow also, with a hundred legs and a length of nearly four inches? Did I tell you I have never heard of an one called "Eulalia"?

W

WU WORLD WOO

▼▼ *{The Who of Wu.}*

If you are to gain a correct impression of how we operate, and how the MerryThought works, you might logically begin with the observation that all of us on Woo possess the same name: Mary Carnivorous Rabbit. Irrespective of age, sex, place of birth, and so forth. This has been the case since time immemorial. We cannot imagine any other way. Furthermore, since some of us live for a very long time, and some of us for only a brief moment or two, the place of time in the MerryThought is vestigial at best. Even what passes for identity on Elmer, or Toutatis, simply has no reality for us here on Wu. My father, Mary Carnivorous Rabbit, once went walking with me in the Garden of Walking Telephones. He said, Mary, there is a thing of great importance which I must reveal to you, a thing which is going to happen to you in your head part. Naturally, Mary, I replied, for it was the truth. I know what you are going to say, ▼▼ 17 father. You are going to say that I am about to have my first experience of Transparency, through the agency of the Woovian Telepathic MerryThought Grid. He looked at me strangely, and was clearly a little puzzled, even a little afraid. It was a quick flash of a look in any case and I, like all Wuvians, am not terribly concerned with analyzing the optic on another's person's feelings. Tough tooty, as the saying goes. Outside of the MerryThought there is little of anything possessive of any intrinsic interest for any of us.

Then, he asked, what am I to do? His confusion seemed quite real; and because he was my father, Mary Carnivorous Rabbit, I let out a little cry of laughter, a suppressed iota of both compression and release, like air going out of a silver signal balloon. Then I clubbed him hard in the face with the stone I had held, secretly, in my fist. He fell backward heavily, and hit the ground flat on his back. The impact was loud and muffled, like the sound of a pillow stuffed with feathers upon the floor. A fine cloud of Silver Woovian dust rose all around his motionless body, and drifted twenty or so meters all about the spot before beginning to slowly settle. The rock was a pretty emerald-streak hunk of raw pyrite, about two and a half pounds. I felt the total lift associated with one's first completed episode of Transparency at that moment, and I must have stood there, rooted like an ancient stone hoodoo, swirling about in the diaphanous netherlight of the MerryThought for four or five years. I know it was quite a long time, for when I finally did come to I stank, was filthy and had soiled the corn-husk and spiderweb gown I had been wearing at my advent. Father's body lay rigid on the silvery sands casting a long, crooked broken-tree-branch shadow over the chilly plain. He had been partly mummified by the dry, slow seasons of Wu. Only the rats or some other pest had made a meal of his face. For the rest, his figure was all twisted up, as though in an ecstasy of some improbable and arcane balletic figure. I smiled as I recalled my advent, my fingers still holding the stone. Before I tossed it away, I searched through the rags I wore, ferreting about for a pocket. When I found one, within my coat, I sank my wiggling fingers deep within, for I was sure I would find a chocolate bonbon hidden somewhere on my person. There it was, with the label of the Hersey Chocolate Company embossed upon it. We do not know what or who a "Hersey" is, but we call all our chocolate by that name, whether it is home-made, or mass-produced in one of our four Woovian chocolate factories (usually two or three of them are closed at any one time for repairs; but this is a laughable practice since no one on Wu has any understanding of how to fix these great, grey, gurgling, rotting machines); or has dropped from a tree, or out of our cloudless sky, or washed up from our one Woovian sea, a tremulous, glittering globule of mercury.

I dropped the stone without much thought, and strode off rapidly down a stretch of the North Paraphrastic Road to see if I could recall where our house was; for I felt a strong desire to see my mother. I also strode the opposite way, because I wasn't too sure which of the two ways was home. Don't forget I was still high as a kite, the first Transparency is always the best.

Rehearsing what I would say, what I would say to my mother, I made my way back, slowly trudging in opposite directions, over the battered, silvery ball of Wu. My mother was a large, fine, stout rhomboid of a woman who wore the standard Woovian costume, a skirt of cornstalks, husks and so forth. The wimple of cheese-cloth, and the wide heavy burnoose of oily rags. Generally, she had the stub of corncob pipe in her mouth. Her name, of course, like mine and father's too, was Mary Carnivorous Rabbit. Her life, unlike mine, has been hard, just after the war. There was not enough to eat. Frequently she had to travel quite far on her old-style Wuvian bicycle to collect a half-dozen spoiled cabbages and over-ripe figs. The remote settlement of Weasel was the only place that still had food markets that were sure to be open. My mother, was a tough old piece of crow, and even the insults of vagabonds, itinerant tinkers and bong farmers along the way did not deter her. I hate to think what might have become of our little family, without her sacrifice. My little brother, Mary Carnivorous Rabbit, was a delicate child and might not have made it had we been forced to endure the fate of the common ▼▼ 19 lot: prolonged and unremitting privation, with no television and limited access to toys, telephones and long stretches when even the MerryThought Grid was down. The nihilist philosopher

Mary Carnivorous Rabbit wrote his or her famous book, *On The Nature Of What Is Said When You Leave The Room,* during this period, and it would not surprise me if the grim, empty and sarcastic tone of that seminal work is a direct result of the unendurable hardships of the times. Certainly the puzzle is not to be solved by a textual examination of the book itself, one of the most maddeningly obscure and complex of the Oracles. The philosopher's biographer however, one Mary Carnivorous Rabbit of the university town of Sensurround, has determined the philosopher's mental age at the time of composition, on the binet scale, as approximately thirty, which happens to be my own age, in centuries.

My younger brother, however, proved a total wastrel when he reached manhood. He incurred a blot upon the family escutcheon, and we don't like to talk about him although it is difficult to avoid the subject altogether owing to the peculiarities inherent in the Wuvian Personal Noun. Mary Carnivorous Rabbit would dawdle on his way home from school, took up dice and gambling, and soon fell in with the wrong crowd. Drugs and petty larceny soon followed. The sad tale is so familiar in these days of loony flip-flap. I recall meeting him myself at the Home for Wayward Boys, and just two weeks prior to the dreadful crime that ended his young life, and our family's joy. Mary seemed composed, repentant and determined to take a new stab at complexity, and the serious responsibilities of adult life. I had brought him a birthday cake, and we shared portions of the messy confection (of course it was a Woovian devils-food cake). I mashed portions of it through the sieve-like wire grate separating offenders from the public. He would fill his cheeks with the stuff, bug out his eyes at me and perch his big, broad Wuvian hands like monstrous but sensitive earflaps, behind his head. I do confess that I got into the spirit of the game, and made some pretty awful faces back, mirroring him. He even took the trouble to push a part of the shapeless, spongy cake back to me, further pulverizing the gooey substance so that it resembled paste rather than pastry. After twenty minutes of this fun one of the guards spotted me and

20

approached. I was taken to a small, windowless room, stripped, scrubbed down by a huge and terrifying female guard with a harelip and a gourd of a goiter who reprimanded me. Appropriately humble and abashed, I was ushered out into the cold, bright meringue of day-time on Woo. It was the last time I ever saw Mary, my brother; for three weeks later, immediately upon his release he wobbled all the way home, indeed half way around the ovoid convolution of Wu, and murdered my mother, Mary Carnivorous Rabbit, in a most atrocious manner. With an implement called a single-knotted Yankee Doodle Electro-flageolet. The dreadful whinny produced by this terrible device is such that a per-son who hears its devilish music with ears unmuffled, or otherwise pro-tected can be expected to expire in a matter of minutes, his or her brains sizzled to a micro-wave frothiness which causes them to spurt from ears, nose and eyes, a steamy horror.

How Mary ever managed to lay hands upon such an evil contrap-tion is a mystery to me, although I suspect one of his knavish fellows in crime at the facility mentioned above. Electro-flageolets, in especial the single-knot variety are very rare; their sole useful purpose is to send shock waves straight to the dwindling molten core of Woo, where occa-sional chunks of hard, unconsumed metalica, or gigacycle plutons called "burps," get awkwardly wedged, throwing the whole world of Wu into the rattling, wild orbital dyspepsia we call "Bill Trousers Hay Ride." But it is no joking matter, since the first effect of even a minor hayride is usually the immediate cessation of the MerryThought. In the more severe episodes of chaotic tumble the gravitational perturbation has been sufficient to launch the unwary Mary Carnivorous Rabbit (caught for instance in an open parking lot with no stable hand-hold or heavy object as support) flinging him or her, literally, off the world. No person so propelled, or rather expelled! into the vacuum of eternal Holy Night has ever been recovered. Traders from Bus, however (a low world of avaricious merchants and tireless hucksters), have reported on quite a few occasions to have found, lost in deep space, solitary Woovian high-tops— battered, daubed with mercury and oil, with shoelaces tied in

▼▼ 21

inextricable knots of the sort only we of Wu know how to do. But why my brother, Mary Carnivorous Rabbit, would enact such a horror must remain for all time a secret since after he dispatched our mother, Mary Carnivorous Rabbit, he wrote an incomprehensible note (which follows) and turned the terrible machine upon his own person, triggering its worm-gear with his own great toe, having removed the sock for better mobility.

Anyway, it was my mother, Mary Carnivorous Rabbit, and not my dead brother, Mary Carnivorous Rabbit, who I wished to speak with on the day I awoke from my very first experience of the Great Transparency, through the psychic good offices of the MerryThought. Moreover, I do believe my mother was still alive at the time, otherwise I wouldn't have tried so hard to find her.

My projected route would take me across parts of Woo not frequently traversed, except by tinkers, Bong Farmers and of course the wanton robbers who have made such a mess of things on our world in recent centuries. Unplugging from the MerryThought grid would leave me untraceable by most of the more commonly used detection devices employed by these ravenous wolves. Unfortunately it would also leave me in a funk, out of sorts and clinically depressed, but being a novice to the greater world of Wu I thought it wise to keep things simple. The trouble was by now I couldn't for the life of me recall exactly where we had lived. Like many Woovians I am much better at navigation when I am going no place in particular. Indeed, when I am going no place in particular, I inevitably find myself bumping into what or whomever it was I did not know I was looking for, but was. This is one of the more delightful qualities of life on Wu, and is the source of frequent misunderstandings between us and the few foreigners who do venture to this clime. Traders from Hamberga mainly, and a few tourists from Japan.

But I reasoned that, having already undergone the primary fission entailed in the Transparency, even if one of us fell victim to the trepidations of the bandittos, one of my semblables would surely make it to my cherished homestead—

where my mom, Mary Carnivorous Rabbit, waited. For being a naturally fissiparous people, we are great guns in the arts of improvisation,
even when we know neither who we are nor what we are doing.

▼▼ ▼▼ *{The Y of Woo.}*

When I was a young girl I had a powerful sense, or intuition, that
when I grew up I would be honored in some way; become widely
known and admired for my actions, my example, or perhaps even for
my wisdom and leadership, like the Majuscule of Wu. I even imagined
I might become the Majuscule of Woo herself. I dreamt of doing the
things she did: she who taught us our name, and how to count; she who
squared the circle of cold, dead primeval Wu, and starting the original
ball bouncing; she who taught us selflessness and how to advance our
people through social amnesia; she who invented the basic outline of
the MerryThought Grid, and taught us to be tamed by our name. Our
name which was, in the beginning, her name. You guessed it: Mary
Carnivorous Rabbit.

She was only a legend among us by the time I was a teenager.
A remote and idolized creature of rumor and myth. Her story was
mingled with every sort of odds and ends of our folklore: the tale of the
Broken Thermometer, Boiled Tom, River Cat and Big Cat, Ying and
Yan, and the story of how the usher of Whydah fructified a conjure-
man's root with the dazzle of Usquebaugh, a dazzle that gave rise to the
shower of William Randolph Trousers and all the muons, pions and
gluons of superfluity, our Woovian curse and holy inheritance.
But in truth did I ever imagine I could be her? No. An impossible dream, yes; a reality, never. Because it was prophesied of
her, Mary Carnivorous Rabbit, the one true Majuscule of Wu,   ▼▼ 23
that only she would circle the square of Woo and accomplish
our collective translation into Dreamtime by traversing every
square inch of Wu. Every single inch. And this knowledge of the

Heavenly Body of Woo would be miraculous and saving. We would emerge from our low and creepy fallen state, and aspire to a higher condition that none of us had ever known, but which had been theoretically limned in a strange Wuvian prophecy called the "Zee of Hare."

Indeed I had not recalled my dream for a long time so engrossed had I become in the delights of Woovian adolescence, petty crime, lust, arson and the free-wheeling joyousness of the young on Wu: revelling in ignorance, contemptuous of their fearful and doddering elders, committed only to babble, lunatic cartwheels; to open mockery of the night sky, and even the ghosts of our kind—victims of Bill Trousers' Hayride, slowly orbiting our gleeful irreverence.

And so it happened, as I released the grip I had maintained for so long on the little ball with which I had dispatched my father, a glitter danced across my face, a glitter as of somethingspeckled shining. An iridescence unknown to gloomy, tedious Woo. I looked more closely at the rock itself, and realized it was the source of this strange radiance. At the same time words echoed in my brain, strange words from the Zee of Hare: "She who gathers gold shall be gatherer, our Initial Unconcealer, against the secret of what is shadowed." Clearly a reference to the identity of the Majuscule of Wu. Clearly the meaning of the verse in question pertained to none other than little me: me, alone of all the myriad inhabitants of Woo, a demigod. But as I stared down at the sacred talisman in the palm of my hand, it began to blur and fade from view. Desperate, I seized and grasped empty air as if an exercise of my will could restore the apparition.

Alas, the truth was I had, like all of my kind on Wu after losing their cherry to the mimble-mamble of the Woovian Telepathic MerryThought Grid, had simply and joyously fissioned; so that I did not know precisely which of my several selves actually possessed the precious object. I sat down, wept, and felt rotten. Surely, if I were truly the Majuscule of Wu I wouldn't be having this problem. If I were Majuscule of Woo I would know all there is to know about the parting of the "Y" and would sense the right fork (if indeed one existed); and would never be

24

troubled by indecision, doubt or a manifest lack of purpose, such as I felt now. Still, Mary Carnivorous Rabbit had her temptations in the desert and so some small uncertainty must have been forgiven her—in her formative years. This thought made me smile. I arose and surveyed the soot-colored bowl of Wuvian sky. The gentle curve of the horizon seemed to glow faintly, the merest vermillion thread of otherworldly neon. I would go, go wherever I must, to encounter myself and find the treasure that would change me, insignificant me—Mary Carnivorous Rabbit—into the fabulous creature I was so sure I already was—Mary Carnivorous Rabbit—The Majuscule of Woo. Surveying what lay before me, the vast salt flat on the outskirts of the town of Rubberneck, a shadow of its former glory, I devised in my mind a recursion pattern, a cycloid:

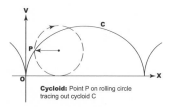

Cycloid: Point P on rolling circle tracing out cycloid C

A cycloid that would enable me, solitarily and severally, in my one-ness and in my multitude, to traverse the entire surface of Wu (after all, not a very big world) in the shortest amount of time, with the smallest aggregate of footsteps. I knew in this manner there would simply be no way possible that I should not encounter my destiny, such as it was.

The trouble was, even after circumambulating the entire surface of Woo I still had not found what it was I was looking for: the corpse of my dear father, Mary Carnivorous Rabbit, and the hunk of raw gold which contained my auspice and constituted my Wuvian lode-stone. Somehow the whole primal scene had vanished from off the surface of the world as though it had never been. Bitterness entered my heart and clouded my soul.

I spent many years by myself, avoiding the mob scene at the clubs and discos of Left Leg, pondering the vanity of Woovian wishes. The work of transparency itself seemed a thing of no worth. For decades I grew bored even with the witless hilarity of the MerryThought Grid itself and could manage no more than a sarcastic sneer at the thought of the idiotic conceit and shallow pleasures of my people. The only book I could stomach was the treatise of the famous nihilist, Mary Carnivorous Rabbit, *On The Nature Of What Is Said When You Leave The Room*. I would go on long walks along stretches of the South Paraphrastic Road reciting long passages aloud, cackling at the wicked cynicism of that dark genius, Mary Carnivorous Rabbit.

One day, while so engaged I happened to look up and was surprised to find myself standing squarely on the pitcher's mound in the middle of the abandoned stadium built millennia ago by whatever people lived on Wu in the olden days, before we arrived. No one grasped its meaning, but strange rumors about ghosts and werewolves caused most of us to give the place wide berth. It was called "John Cheese's Mouse-trap" and, like I say, was not considered a proper place to stumble upon, much less hang out at. In my current state of thorough abjection I simply had not noticed where my feet were taking me—I had been mulling over one of the more obscure epigrams from Mary Carnivorous Rabbit's book:

> Close the drapes.
> Aunt Wednesday
> is changing.

I had been worrying, in fact, for a period of several years about this saying and just couldn't quite get the sense of it, when I happened to look up and realize where I was. It seemed quite a Woovian joke on me, and I think I must have laughed inwardly because outwardly I smiled, at least so I am told by my teammates, as we came to reconstruct the whole story a long time later during the seventh inning stretch while playing a team of Bong farmers at a ballpark near the Garden of Walking Telephones.

Anyway, what happened on that fateful Wuvian afternoon—it was a Wednesday as I recall—must have had something to do with the epigram from the Nihilist's book, *On The Nature Of What Is Said When You Leave The Room.* As my mood lightened and lifted ever so slightly, I was doubly stunned to notice a band of my semblables, fractional phantoms of the fissioning process, beckon and come towards me, all dressed in identical costumes, though each sported a distinct insignia emblazoned on the breast. These I later learned were called "numbers" and though of no use whatever on Woo (where identity is more often expressed in terms of blur) proved useful in playing the game they set about showing me. Other tools of leather, wood and other alien substances seemed initially baffling to me until they were explained by one Mary Carnivorous Rabbit a bit more "with it," as they say, than the rest. Before long we were all merrily engaged in this new pastime, and our shouts and cries of delight echoed through the empty stadium for the first time in perhaps a million years. I had come out of my blue funk.

▼▼ ▼▼ ▼▼ *{The Otherwho of Wu}*

[Asterism]: My Brother Mary Carnivorous Rabbit's Suicide Note:

> *Dear Mary Carnivorous Rabbit,*
>
> *May I call you "Mary"? I hope so, Mary, because I feel the need to unburden my soul to one who will understand, understand better than I, what it is I need to unburden myself of; for it is a mystery to me. For the world of Woo weighs heavily upon me even though it is a small, dark, measly world. And the weight of the crime I have committed weighs heavily upon me even though I* ▼▼ 27 *feel no particular remorse, as I am not even convinced I know why I have done this act which rests heavily upon my brow like... like the exploded view of a marine steam engine connecting*

rod, in three states: A) assembled B) disassembled: 1, connecting rod; 2, strap; 3, brass; 4, gib; 5, cotter. And thirdly: pulverized, or reduced to dust and powder and dispersed as a pungent, semi-noxious aerosol, as a loathsome fume. Indeed, the moralist within, which is the captain of my soul, cannot even comprehend the Evil which is alleged to have transpired, as agented by the lower organs of the body, the arm and body parts, always mutinous, fidgety and prone to Error and Monkeyshines; in all respects incompatible with the theoretical self, which I, Mary Carnivorous Rabbit, have caused to be erected as a public monument to the better class of Wuvian idea and persiflage. Who knows what Evil lurks below, in the sub-cellar of the Woovian heart? Who knows who of you, and you, and you… my semblables and otherwhos have not gathered by the same unholy campfire and feasted on the same forbidden barbecue? Is the Wuvian soul not like a micro-miniature of precious gold we work upon with our pathetic microliths of conscience in a vast, dark emptiness where we are forced to play crack the whip, lit only by the microlux of our Woovian wherewithal? Alone. Aghast. Ashen-assed.

Remember me when you think on the ewe-necked ewer of your own malfeasance, all curve and evolute—the locus of the centers of curvature of, or the envelop of the normals to, another curve.

Sincerely, your brother and otherwho,

Mary C. R.

UU

► *{Ravenello, or Doctor Ravenello}:*

Ideas, someone said, are dime a dozen—unless you don't have one. Was it Eulalia? Could have been, I suppose. Knowledge of things like the question has a way of hiding, hiding just beyond the hillock there, covered with bluish-green dust and what look like balls of yarn; an isle of the sublime in a wilderness of witless reflection. You can call me 萝卜 .[2] That's something in the Chinese language, a language I do not pretend to understand. It's not a real name anyway, only a provisional one, since I wouldn't know what to call myself if I possessed a real name, or names; further, I'm not sure I'd know what a real name is, or how to differentiate one from a false name, or a box nail, or even an ordinary narration.

You can also call me Ravenello, or Doctor Ravenello for short.

► 31

Now, if I heard myself say something about Eulalia being

---

[2] ideogram for radish

at one time present here, it is probably a fact. I only know about what is from what I do, and say. And see, despite the terrible brightness. Since on the world of 1965UU there is no hard and fast distinction between saying and doing, my mind is at ease with regards to the sanctity of the factual. The factuality of Eulalia, I mean. She with her wavy abundance of golden locks and fire eyes and harp. I think it is a harp. Or maybe a horp. But that's as far as I am willing to go. For once I was, aha, I was in love with another one of us, a one of us (or them) called Rosalind. I first read her name on a box of chocolates that I found on the beach near the town of Hessian Crucible, a wedge and a half past the pyramid of Whatsisname the Chiropractor. You know, the guy with the problem of random motion golfballs and left-eyed needles. Rosalind remembered me from a dream of some former place, but never seemed quite sure of who it was. This is called the Plato Plate Tectonic Theory of love and is a good place to squirrel away your pennies, even if they are bad ones. She too like Eulalia possessed a euphonious name and golden locks of way-out waviness. A waviness I never noticed until it was pointed out to me by a skunk named O'Ryan who collected, as I recall, tinsel, and was rumored to be descended from a happy and accidental conjunction of the fabulous Polo Bear and a certain notorious lightbulb.

Rav, she said and I think she meant it, for that was all she said. She henceforth walked away, her pink scarf whispering like the line a quill makes on paper while its finger is thinking, thinking on love. Love or its hearsay. Love or its heresy. Both kinds implicit. Both kinds of implicitness fully explicit here on 1965UU because what is evident is far from feeling so, as our little world topples through the void like a hedgehog (what's that?) through the crabgrass. And I don't know what that is either, although there is said to be a patch of it growing some way from here, down the path a little, near the Bad Place which scares me. But I'm not up to visiting places that scare me, so I make a rule of avoiding it along with its theoretical crabgrass.

1965UU is an M-type metallic planetoid. That means among other things it possesses a very high albedo. Albedo is the measure of reflectivity of an object, an object floating in the emptiness of whatever there is to float about in, a question that has never interested me, or my kind. We would call ourselves the Whatsisnames if we had an occasion to do so, but we don't so we don't. High Albedo means that 1965UU is a very bright world, probably because it is a very smooth one. To transit the entire world, only fourteen miles across at its widest and slightly less than seven, at its thinnest, requires only a flick of the wrist. And what we call a Double Uvian Push-Off Spike to shove off from. Otherwise if you move too fast you just fall down, fall down flat on your face. And to complicate the matter you must needs push off from one of a class of somethings called Prehistoric (whatever that is, since we possess no "history" whatever that is, but only hearsay, hearsay of two types, but more of that later) Cast-iron Mississippi Deep-Embedded Bottle Openers (or DEBOs) of which there are only forty-nine on the entire surface of the world. Suffice it to say, the wonders of travel and exploration possess little in the way of allure for most of us. The smooth, impossible slicketyness of our homeland and the incredible glare (we must all wear shades when not deep in the umbra of her darkest velvety nightshadow) make even ordinary daily excursions extraordinarily complex crises in nerve management. Virtually all of us, Alphonse and Rosalind included, are chronically banged up and the victims of the sort of chronic lower-back syndrome you find only on the most tortured and neurotic worlds, Roswitha for instance, or Shikoku. You know, the place where everyone sits around all day at his or her own grand piano playing chopsticks over and over. Oh, I forgot, Albedo is also Alphonse Bedo, second cousin once removed and a tense rival for Rosalind's affections, if you can call them that since her habitual pattern of dropping in an out of people's live is so chronically un-Double-Uvian as to mark her as a rare sort   ► 33
of aberration among us. A Double-Uvian Rarebit. Still Rosalind is adored by many, despised by many, by reason of her

uncanny ability to discover whenever need arises the DEBO of greatest proximity, and the agility to shove off from any of these with the aid of a long silver darning needle she keeps with her at all times. We suspect, or some of my comrades suspect (I am an ingenuous being and thus quite incapable of suspicion), that somehow Rosalind had either come across (or glided upon, which would be more accurate on our slickety little planetoid) or, even more unimaginably yet, had even gone so far as to invent a mappamundo or geographical chart of the entirety of 1965UU. Since we imagine the place to be shaped more or less like a Klein Bottle, and thus near the border of definable non-entity and verifiable single dimensionality, this was a crazy supposition. But, what with her world-class flash and whiz, she and I rarely had time to exchange a word or two beyond the most basic pleasantries. So much for communication, in any case communication as it is customarily construed. Indeed, owing to the peculiarities of the place and how we have evolved—evolved I guess is the word (which depends far more on, well, on attitude than on the sharing of deep, inner feelings and the like)— it could be said we have remained, in some senses, clueless. But since we live on a world of absolute nocturnal opacity alternating with an alien state of glare so deep it feels almost a living thing, feelings and the like, convivial sharing of life's little joys and heartbreaks, seem to many of us a lot of malarkey; not to mention a real danger given our pronounced propensity, despite all the best efforts, to fall down, busting our asses thereby, when we do find ourselves in the tremulous grip of real emotion. Feelings: a throwback to the mythical time of Eulalia and the other moths, when the solar system as it was known was thought to be a unified cultural field, a veritable constitutional mockery.

► ► *{The Name That Was Too Much}*:

They say, by the way, that it was Eulalia who gave us our name, only I am not too clear on the exact identity of this "they". Like many things on 1965 UU the precise nature of its status, qua thing, remains obscure. Al Bedo and I would quarrel frequently over this and related issues even before the matter of Rosalind arose, or skidded past like a mirage; pulchritude in transit, seemingly impossible to possess. Al Bedo is short and squat whereas I am tall and lanky, and so our attempts at fisticuffs generally resulted in a rude and humiliating comedy of wildly mistimed jabs and uppercuts, and consequent to these, sudden and frequently painful falls and awful tumbles. Awful falls and thumpings with loud concussive reports. In those days I was called Umbria, and was known for my sad and melancholy disposition. Indeed, for several years in succession I was unofficial Poet Laureate of the entire South Temperate Zone, a place congenial to the waxing and waning of my poetical temperament owing to the relative infrequency of visits there by my nemesis and rival, Monsoor Bedo, the swine. When I first fell in love with Rosalind I composed the following poem:

> Rosalind,
> Rosalind,
> Rosalind
> bright as a pin.
> Pin, pin, pin, pin.

But she would rush by with such celerity that invariably I never was able to get the whole thing out while she remained in earshot. Still, Al Bedo would sometimes surprise me, and mock my sentimental musings by giving me the raspberry or other insults too gross to relate. In this circumstance the inevitable fisticuffs would result, with the usual inglorious and painful outcome— ► 35 the two of us wiggling about like bugs on still water, arms and legs flailing in helpless disarray.

What Rosalind made of all of this is difficult to ascertain as I never caught more than a glimpse of her heavenly features as she whisked by, bright as a pin indeed. I do not suppose she can fail to have noticed me, sensitive and remote with my shades and look of dark brooding. Perhaps she was too involved in some extraordinary Nolooky, a Nolooky she had cunningly committed to memory; though this latter possibility seems a highly improbably one as the committing of any text (whatever that is) or any other sort of information of consequence is expressly forbidden by an ancient rule. Our only rule, in fact: Qwaklaklaklaklakafordoomeddedumheofshepinpinpinklakakladoctor-ravenello (What ever is is perforce forbidden).

In fact, the original name of our world might have been Uttermost or Utah-Uxmal or simply Utter Stutter; but whatever the name of it was, that name of it came to be universally regarded, or otherwise adumbrated, as The Name That Was Too Much, and so fell into disuse except by only a churlish few, a churlish few known only to themselves and their fellows as The Society of the Undershot Waterwheel (named for a local architectural oddity and relic from the remote Unrecorded Undershot past). This society consisted of three acolytes and a Master, and possessed collectively the extreme variety of Nolookys on the whole world. These acolytes were: Monsoor Bedo, myself and Rosalind, although her membership was mostly an honorific since she never attended any of the meetings, except once or twice when she came rocketing through, upsetting our Mystic Ratchets and Pentacles, our Template of Gold and Crowns of Silver. In spirit she was with us, we felt sure. I suppose I was already thinking on reconfiguring myself in the form and under the rubric of Doctor Ravenello, for even at this time my thoughts were like tattered silk, or like a whole clothesline of lingerie buffeted by the light breeze of a May morning (whatever that is).

Nolookys, by the way, are our interior theater wherein are enacted any conceivable drama or comedy or theatrical, and this without any instrumentality since, aside from our Pushing

Sticks, darning needles and BEDOS, we have no technological artifacts of any kind. One initiates a Nolooky simply by glancing at pages from a text of the script to be enacted. These texts are to be found scattered about everywhere on 1965 UU like great, ungainly fowl, geese or ducks. The monthly winds we call "The Censor's Hand" blows these up from regions we know not. It is a mystery, like the sudden appearance of moths in an unknown closet.

Glance at, rather than read, I must stress; since to actually read a text is forbidden also as a corollary of our one rule because of the nearness of reading to the act of committing to memory. Or one may think of each of these odd behavitives as stages on life's little way, just as the drinking of milk and the inhalation of the Furred Ragweed on Mahoney is said the prepare one for fullblown crystal meth addiction. Nolookys came into fashion sometime during the last century owing to the obvious deterioration of our theater. No one knows who first called them "Nolookys", but the name stuck, or stuck as much of anything is capable of sticking on the slickety slicks of 1965 UU, a world devoid of stickum.

Our leader and Supreme Hydriotaphian, he who wields the Urim and Thummin, and the Urinalist of our woes was one Umberto the Polisher, who is a previous life had been the originator of what is called the Modified John Simon, a receptacle wherein we pass water when we pass water. There is some uncertainty about all of this, be it hearsay or heresy, because several others including Monsoor Bedo claim to be the original originator of the Modified John Simon. Monsoors Hoole and Boole as well, the fooles. And, while we are on the subject, would it be out of place for me to mention I also harbor some recollection of that most remarkable invention? And there is an odd lapse in my past, a lapse that occurred at roughly the period during which the Origination, in point of fact, originated. A coincidence? Let Modesty smile on my silence, just as does History from her ► 37 marble cranny, somewhere, in the deep interior regions of our little world. Now Umberto the Polisher guided us with great gentleness and great strictness. His gentleness was of the strictest, and his gentility all stricture. Reputedly, it was he who in the Olden Times taught Rosalind to play the horp, and her hair how to curl up wave upon wave as the gold gathered the light against it, pound by pound. He was a perfectionist by trade and thus unfit by training or temperament to be indwelling upon our little world, U—as it was called, the place with The Name That Was Too Much. For whenever he came across one of our rough spots or passages in those days (rough spots, basins or passages were quite, quite common), the hillocks covered with bluish-green dust and balls of yarn (whatever that is) he would set about polishing, polishing, polishing. Polishing with cunning abrasives mined in the ancient quarries near Urk and Jerk. He made a practice of doing this polishing, polishing, polishing behind our backs so that in truth it was clandestine polishing; polishing of a perhaps shameful sort that so obsessed our Grand Hydriotaphian with his Urim and Thummim. Had we been wiser, Monsoor Al Bedo, that swine, and my delectable yet wholly unattainable Rosalind, we might have grown wise to the fact before it became act. But no, Al and I quarreled and changed names and engaged in senseless fisticuffs as the world grew brighter and brighter and brighter. And Rosalind whizzed and whizzed, as resistless to the skin of 1965 UU as the most perfect of semiconductors. All of us resorting, day by day, to thicker and thicker shades to dull the fierce, devouring glare. Umberto had decided to make our world as perfect a place as possible given the fact it was shaped like a Klein Bottle. Not only did this monumental hubris involve the polishing, polishing, polishing of her raw metallica to a fineness capable of an astounding albedo (reflectivity, you will recall); but also the elision, the final and full elision of The Name That Was Too Much and this despite the fact that we in the Society of the Undershot Waterwheel had dedicated our lives to the preservation of this name; consecrated our lives to its ineffable essence, as well as this name's tendency to whiffle—to flicker, to flutter, rather like a swath of tattered silk.

I discovered Umberto the Polisher's true motive one day at the town of Tutu Bryght (named by a rascal named Fried Harvey in sardonic response to our global brightening). I was relieving myself at a portable Modified John Simon luck had conveniently placed nearby, when I happened to hear a voice, a voice engaged in the recitation of a poem. Rosalind, it began:

> Rosalind.
> Rosalind,
> Rosalind,
> Rosalind,
> with golden thread
> on one end.

It was the deep basso of our Supreme Hydriotaphian; and in truth, there she was, faintly discernable flittering along the horizon, somewhere far off, probably totally zonked out on the narcotic (and unconstitutional) Nolooky she had memorized, the poor deluded girl. Clearly (whatever that means) Umberto the Polisher possessed a hidden agenda, and that agenda had something to do with Rosalind. Only what could it possibly be?

Could it be _____? No, not that!

I pushed the horrid thought out of my mind, and pushed off with a fugitive Double Uvian Pushing Spike I had bartered my last pair of clean socks for, and began to sail lightly around the moebius-equator of our world, the wind fluttering in my locks in a demonic disarray. It seemed a long time since I had relaxed in this manner, but I figured I needed to chill out a bit, recollect myself to myself and besides walking had become difficult of late owing to an unpleasant, sharp, piercing pain in my backside; no doubt stress related.

In the fury of my initial push off, I did not realize that ► 39 jealousy over Umberto the Polisher's possible interest in... no, no, push, push it out... had given me close to superhuman (whatever that is) strength. Indeed, the DEBO I had shoved off from had fused with the prong of my spike and had been literally torn off the surface plate of 1965 UU's glittering metallica; my career was torrid, maniacally fast and uttermostly thrilling. Being a typical 1965 Double Uvian I had experienced little in the way of thrill except for that of attitude, the habit of slinking around being cool, man, too cool for words.

But this was something else, this was something hot. I began to see what it must've been like to be, well, to be in the body of Rosalind. There might be something to be said for never keeping still, never settling down, never putting down roots as they say. Especially on our world that possesses a silvery skin so hard it is next to impossible to nick, much less dent. And there was something to be said for simply, wickedly, unabashedly flashing past whomsoever, flashing as fast as... as the slicketyness of the place would permit. Rosalind, I began to perceive was not your average skirt, was not your average pretty face; she was a pretty face with a mind.

I had pretty much traversed the entire place—I had in fact traversed the entire place because I arrived, briefly, at the point or near it, for plainly visible there was the ragged, torn up hole, where my spike had jerked the BEDO right out of the ground. Umberto would be furious, for I had done the scratchy upon his slicketyness. But since the occasion of the horrid thought I had pushed off from, or rather pushed out of my mind, I was frankly not so sure about him. My skepticism, not shared by my nemesis, that... that... that blockhead, extended to the question of the rightness of honoring as Supreme Hydriotaphian one such as Umberto whose relentless polishing was liable to be viewed as a direct cause of the global white-out so clearly evident, even in the Nolooky-free Hidden Zone of Dunbar's Egg, near Kandahar. Even Polish Hat, near the North Polar Region, formerly a place of gloomy arctic fogs and mists, had become almost as bright as places like the Heliotrope Amphitheater, a sun worshipper's mecca near the racetrack. Even with the majesty of his Urim and Thummin, Umberto had become, for me at least, one whose name is too, too much. A candidate for erasure. And yet, and yet. As I thought on this I chattered my teeth; as I chattered my teeth I considered whether to change my name. Each time I change my name, the ideas spill out of me like flour from a flour sack and I am reduced to care.

So I did not change my name.

If Umberto the Polisher was a fraud, and Rosalind an apparition, what must I do? If a ceaseless changing of names appeared to be the only evolution I could expect; and if even the world under my feet possessed no reliable moniker, was there any reason left not to despair? I probably would have succumbed to exactly that morbid fate had I not noticed out of the corner of one eye, out of the very corner of that corner, the slow, puffing, wheezing figure of Alphonse Bedo, my antagonist. For of late he had taken to haunting me, following from a safe distance (I still carried the Pushing Spike mentioned above and was a dangerous man) making unpleasant noises, daring me to approach, mocking me and occasionally even pelting me with stones and rotten fruit.

As I came close to total despair, a piece of prehistoric merd flung presumably by my ancient foe caught me square in the middle of the forehead, and I temporarily left my body—a rare thing on 1965 UU since we have always had, from time immemorial, last week that is, a difficult time focusing our mental energy on any specific thing or task. Not quite conscious, not quite unconscious, I drifted seemingly up and out of the sad spot of my unfortunate beaning. I watched as Al Bedo approached, poked at me with his foot and then went through my pockets; for a moment it seemed he might hoist me on my own petard; but no, after making several menacing feints he merely filched my Pushing Spike, and lumbered off in the direction of Christmas County, a region of rusting tube alloys and other ► 41 junk avoided even by Umberto the Polisher. A place sacred to madmen. His much inferior spike he left with me.

No doubt Alphonse, too, had hopes of courting Rosalind; I cared not. Somehow all my former life seemed empty and silly. I found my lips pronouncing the words: Qwaklaklaklaklakafordoomeddedumheof-shepinpinpinklakakladoctorravenelowaswastaningstandingstillsok-lakastill (What ever is is perforce forbidden unless it is at stand still). The odd sentence kept repeating in my mind until I realized it was our first rule, but a version of our first rule I had never heard. And what I had never heard was particularly the last part... stonden still. In a blinding moment of revelation I realized what I must do, for indeed there was no way I would ever catch up with Rosalind so quick was she. Quick, quick, full of holy quickness. After decades of trying we had exchanged only a word or two. A few tiresome cliches about the weather and the glare. But now, in my illuminated state, I realized that whatever name I took made no difference as long as I observed the unfashionable rule of my own quixotic nature, and stood still. Stood still, and awaited Rosalind; for come she must, sooner or later. There was no question of that. I had simply been pursuing the incorrect tactic, an especially incorrect tactic for 1965 UU because its shape dictates that all vectors run into, and are completed at, every point—except for the occasional hillock of ruined tube alloys (remnants of the Big Boom Eulalia spoke of?) covered with bluish-green dust, and balls of what looks like yarn.

► ► ► *{Hearsay or Heresy}:*

Such was the fervor of my newly illuminated soul that the future became clear to me, or what became clear to me was a bifurcation (a double U, so to speak) of the river of Wild Time into two distinct torrents of probability. The first I shall call a Future Hearsay, and it runs roughly thus:

Through fasting and meditation, I learn to overcome my deep-rooted problem. This I accomplish by the following simple method. I apply an amber drop of honey to the tip of my nose, and focus on it, thereby becoming at first cross-eyed, and consequently enlightened (why does this sound familiar?). I also become a sort of public monument; humble penitents come from miles around to lay wreaths at my feet, along with votive candles and burnt offerings. Butterflies and young wasps are attracted to the sweet nectar on my proboscis. After a considerable period of time various legends, mostly inaccurate or incomprehensible are elaborated to explain me. Some of these are very touching, such as that of the bard Meander whose verses proclaim me a rare fruit or melon, a gift from the gods of remote antiquity in return for an unspecified act of generosity on the part of the Old Ones, our ancestors who slept in big clay jars and played the ocarina. But through all of this I am conscious, silently singing over and over my little song:

> Rosalind,
> Rosalind,
> Rosalind,
> Rosalind,
> pretty as a pin.
> Pin, pin, pin, pin.

One day I see a slight commotion on the edge of the world, on the lip of that far away metallica where all our doubts are devoured by the endless wonder of illimitable night, Eulalia's starry gown. I know what it is, and a wise half-smile crinkles the corners of my mouth. For it is Rosalind speeding along the Great Circle of her perfect freedom, coasting along in perfect accord with my lover's calculation. The inevitable is about to be enacted, as I had hoped.

From afar I can just make out the joy of joy, or surprise, or ► 43
horror (it cannot be horror can it?) on her perfect physiognomy. Because she now sees the future, me that is, rapidly approach-

ing. I am a destiny now, perhaps one she had given up as lost, impossible, a hope faded by the harsh wind of hard fact, and

Whack! I am knocked a country mile, am spun through the Double Uvian glare like a billiard ball, knocked silly despite the sweet rapture of my bliss, the long bliss of standing still. When I come to, I notice Rosalind lying quietly nearby, her aviator's cap beside her and a goose-egg on her delicate forehead. I apply ointment and rare medicines to her wound and shortly she is revived. She looks upon me with new eyes and she awakens to her new life as my betrothed. We embrace.

Later, after our nuptials and brief honeymoon near the vacation resort at Nova Melinda, I take on a new identity as Norman Normal, a breaker of rocks in the Abrasion Quarries at Blimp Town, a happening place. I, Norman Normal, is, am, a woof, as is my bride, Rosalind Normal; we raise our young woofs according to the ancient First Rule: Qwaklaklaklaklakafordoomeddedumheofshepinpinpinklakakladoctorravenellowaswastandingstandingstillsoklakastill; our seedlings are scattered to the wind and a new population is popped, for all time. For all to marvel upon. A popcorn of population, a popcorn of woofs. Even in times of durance when the vicious wind blows in, flowing with crows.

► ► ► ► *{Heresy, Not Hearsay}:*

The second branch of my probabilitarian prolusion is as distinct as the above, yet unlike it, distinctly disturbing. Hence its anathematization.

In this version Error enters the world, enters in the form of a slight wrinkle, or lumpum. All proceeds exactly as in ► ► ►

up to the Whack! as recorded some pages above. In this disturbing version a small wrinkle, or lump, on the surface of 1965 UU causes poor Rosalind to part ways from her perfect trajectory and careen off, wildly and tragically coming so close only to miss me, her theoretical beloved, by the merest smidgen, by a proverbial hair's-breadth; instead she goes rocketing off into the nullity of Missed Opportunity. And I am lost, become a tuna-head of folly and hopelessness. For some moments I simple stand there unable to believe what has happened. Close examination of the lump reveals to me that the seeds of my folly reside in the incompetence of Umberto the Polisher. The "if only" shall torment me forever I realize, and break out in quacks of dry, soulless mirth.

Gradually I, the person formerly known as "Doctor Ravenello", formerly known as "Umbria", transforms into a vacant lump of soapstone, a true monument now, but a monument of no use even to vagabond storytellers and Gypsies. Passing animals urinate in my face, chunks of me are pulled off by juvenile delinquents, and irreverent riflemen employ me as the object of target practice. Aeons pass and Umberto the Polisher, Alphonse Bedo and even my fair Rosalind are nothing but so much bluish-green dust and what looks like balls of yarn. My fate has become an endless Nolooky of no consequence. A Nolooky known to none. My silly wishes are like what pours down the porcelain throat of a Modified John Simon; and the double U of this world seems only an ironic double-cross too, too difficult to bear.

You decide which.

▶ ▶ ▶ ▶ ▶ *{A Textual Uttermost: Being a Tractatus Upon the Wherefore of Why We Possess No Stickum; On the Sliding Off of Names and Other Scary Messes}:*

Sometimes I look up at the sky and discover a certain wonderful peace. All the time I have wasted on futile things gives me pause to pause, and think it over. Life is short, even in the Nolooky of linked analogies; a pretty face, like that of Rosalind, offers the lie to knowability, even to the possibility of stickum itself.

Still I can imagine other worlds, and other outcomes; places like Linda Susan and such, where people are able to enjoy the fruit of the vine. Because the name of the vine is fixed and does not wiggle off, or become "rhinoceros" while you are in the middle of your enjoyment.

I am reminded of an old story I recall from my youth; I was called Silver Bear then and lived with my family at a place called Chrome Dome. We made a living operating a toll gate on the one major highways connecting the dark, hidden part of 1965 UU with the rest of it. I had a sister, a fine young, flaxen haired girl named Melody. One day Melody ran into, literally, an old woman at the crossroads leading to the long deserted Mansion of Ushk, a scary place rumored to be haunted by unknown spirits of great malevolence, bats and creepy Thorns and Eths, intellectual fungi and other creepy stuff. Once both had recovered they engaged in much profound conversation concerning the higher things, at least according to Melody, who forgot to take notes and so forgot it all, silly duck. But somewhat later this strange woman took out her glass eye, and gave it to my sister to hold. The old woman's eye delighted Melody so much she decided to run off with it, which she did. But after she got home she regretted her crime and confessed. Our father wanted to return the eye, as he was always quite scrupulous about business ethics. Mother, on the other hand, thought the eye was an extraordinary object of wonderment, and supposed it would bring us good luck. We talked the matter over all night, and finally decided we would keep the eye, but give the old woman something in return. I suggested a radish from our garden, one of the bright, reddish and roundy radishes of the Small Worlds of which we are so proud.

I was chosen to select the radish, which I did with very great care, choosing a nearly spherical one that was nearly as beautiful as the Old Woman's eye. She was waiting at the crossroads, as if she knew I was coming. I bowed low and without a word offered her the radish. She bowed low and took it, covering her face with a tattered shawl; then she did something—

something I did not see—with her scrawny fingers. Something so quick and complicated her fingers were a blur, a wonder of fingers. I saw she had replaced radish for eye, and stranger yet the radish now so much resembled an eyeball that I could not tell which eye was eye, and which was radish. I was very much delighted by all this and asked the old woman, how could this be?

Things will go where they belong if they are allowed to, she said and bowed low. She said: Even names of the highest things, and of the beloveds, they go where they belong. Not understanding, I bowed low and ran home. We looked under Melody's calico pillow, where she had secreted the old woman's eye. There, there was the radish, vividly vermillion, all roundy and perfect.

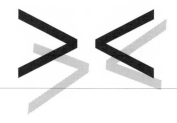

MITAKE—MURA

● *{ How It All Began}:*

It all started when one of us, I forget which one, suggested we banish all hereditary titles and declare a Radical Republic. It might have been Z'huq; it might have been El Pez Que Fuma, or it might even have been me, The one who goes by the name of Twin Donuts. The truth is, I am not sure. And in any event it doesn't matter since once the whole sequence started, it took on a life belonging to no other tribe, achieved what is caused critical infarction and, thus, constituted a new thing, a new thing beyond the ken of any of us. Something new in the slow unfolding of human affairs had begun. But I am ahead of myself. For here on the little world of Mitake Mura, we have adapted to the whirl and white wrath of Eulalia; we have not opposed her comings and goings with the erection of foolish monuments, culture and art, wars and commerce, no. We ride on the wriggle of Time's dot as it rides on, on and on forever, through the murky cloud of our sister worlds, all apparently very much alike—like this place, humble Mitake Mura as she hugs the meaningless

● 49

self-identity of her orbit, always herself, always perfect.

The dancing dot of the present we Mitake Murans, all three of us, call the "*Rose", even though the word has no meaning for us, and few associations of the conventional kind. The *Rose is an ultimate authority, and so we structure our lives around its dulcet fragrance. All our silly lives, full of vainglory and misguided passion, comprise, according to the unspoken rule, the metaphysical airy disc of the *Rose, or the visible airy disc of its quite invisible dot. So our lives here on this two mile hunk of pyrite and chrysoprase revolve around this dot, this dot which is and then is no more. And so, from a detached point of view our work is simple. We dot, dot, and re-dot; we dot, dot and re-dot the rune of the world's ruins. Eulalia knew this, and that is why, perhaps, she never returned. The dot of her coming passed, and shall never be again. The dot of her Second Coming is a re-dot we shall deal with at some point, but there is no point in worrying the question with a false wriggle of surmise. Only the "*Rose", flower of its own fragrance dots and re-dots the "i" of our human surprise. We expect no more, or so we did up until a certain point upon which I shall, all in good time, fully expatiate, if that is the right word.

First, let me scenarioize the set of my theatrical, the world of Mitake Mura. Mitake Mura is a smallish irregularly shaped chunk of chrysoprase, chalcedony as it used to be called, and some stray pyrites. All the nickel oxide makes it somewhat greenish in appearance, but I only know that from what I've read in one of the old faxes, several millions of dot before the *Rose, and speeding away even as we speak, or as I speak to be slightly more correct. Not that mere correctness matters much to me; the past is flying down its mystic coal shute so rapidly that matters of correctness, decorum and consistency and such, have traditionally had little importance for us.

Still, one day not so long ago Z'huq and I were watering

the mangy lawn that surrounds the crappy tin-roofed shack that contains our fax-machine and is also the only dwelling on the entire world, when El Pez Que Fuma came staggering out waving and grimacing.

It has come to life, it has come to life! he announced.

Now none of us knew what a fax machine was for anymore. Only, it looked neat beneath the swaying 60 watt bulb, perched on its little, square table. So we made a habit of dusting it regularly, oiling its secret parts, and religiously keep the thing plugged into the single wall socket on the wainscotting of the north wall within the shed (bad storms had broken the windows of the south and east walls, so it was all we could do, what with our measly supply of tacks and stapled grease-paper to keep out the seasonal winds, whatever they are).

It has come to life, and paper is scrolling out. Paper with something written on it. Hey, this is a miracle, a bona fide act of the Unseen! Z'huq, Twin Donuts, what should we do?

Neither of us had a clue either, although strictly speaking it was none of our business, for procedural reasons. According to our ancient and imperishable rule there was but one Grand Imperial Master of the Shed, although this role rotated in shifts, three to the term of a single Mitake-Muran day and sister night. For instance, when I was Shed Master, Z'huq and El Pez Que Fuma would serve as First and Second Cheese Masters; when Z'huq was Shed Master, El Pez Que Fuma and I would serve as First And Second Cheese Masters; and, of course, when El Pez Que Fuma began his term as Shed Master, Z'huq and I once more were relegated to the lowly and nearly meaningless task of Cheese Master (there is no cheese on Mitake-Mura; we don't know what a "cheese" is, and wouldn't recognize it if one walked right up to any of the three of us, bowed low, and said, "How do you do?" in the most fluent Mitake-Muran.

This regular alternation of titles, as I have noted, has been traditional with us from time immemorial—at least to Dot before *Rose. Our ancient rule was like all true innovation, a child of necessity, as the shed itself was too small to hold more

● 51

than one comfortably, and contained only one moth-eaten sleeping bag rolled up on the shelf next to the door. The Radical Republic, I am proud to say, was my idea. It just seemed foolish to us for such a hierarchy to persist; why not build an addition to the shed? Besides, the role of Cheese Master is an absurd one given the fact that there is no such thing as cheese. And finally, why should we not enjoy the fruits of librery, fraternitussle, equalitude and thus cease from our relentless, witless abuse and habit of terrorizing each other and each in turn, Z'huq, El Pez Que Fuma and Twin Donuts, as we assume the terrible and absolute dominion of Shed Master? I had at the time not heard of Democritus (and all the other demos), Pericles—nor Gerard Winstanley, Voltaire, Anarchasis Cloots, Robespierre, Bakunin, Andrew Jackson, Jefferson, not even Linda Susan—so I flatter myself on my happy political intuition. If intuition it was; for my secret thought has always been that I am a genius, full head and shoulders above, in the great scheme of things, my low and mediocre countrymen. Who among them could have dreamed democracy? Miserable Z'huq? He is incapable of latching the shed door, and never folds and packs away the sleeping bag with customary elegance; furthermore he is a timid sort, afraid of risks and novelty. El Pez Que Fuma assures me Z'huq has never been to the North Pole of Mitake-Mura because of his fear of unsteady places, and the North Pole is pitched upon an outcropping high above a gulf beneath which flows endless night, the abode of devils, bats and other nameless horrors. El Pez Que Fuma is a lot more fun to hang out with, but is prone to cross-dressing when presiding as Shed Master, and is hopelessly addicted to the greasy pitch which is to be found congealed in the pits that occur in the Karst regions of the South Temperate Zone. Sometimes he (she) comes traipsing back dragging his (her) wilted ball gown, half covered in soot, for all the world like a demented doll half in blackface, capricious, unpresentable, and a total disaster as a public figure and image of authority.

52

All this was tried before, the fax read, and all this failed miserably. Humankind can create nothing. The fax was unsigned, except with the strange legend, Minus GigaDot Before *Rose, apparently a claim to temporal priority. A fax from the past, in fact. Was I ever stunned. It is your fault, stammered El Pez Que Fuma, his blear eyes quaking on their twin eye-stalks beneath the faded lace of his soiled wimple. Still too stunned, I was unable for a moment to reply. Then, however, a rage seized me: You have suborned my authority as Shed Master and disrupted the natural flow—what we call the Normal Vronksian Perambulation of Dots; not to mention pre and post-dots as they adorn the sanctum of the *Rose, you plebeian fiend. I hereby order you to be decapitated and drownded in honeybear amber. Z'huq, go and bring the axe from its nail on the old oak tree.

At this point (or rather, dot of the *Rose) the bright scarlet bead of the fax machine changed to green, and the typical rushing whir and rattle of fax talk silenced our merely human squabble. This time three full pages, this time from a spacetime far, far off in the future—nearly ten plus GigaDots after the *Rose. Even El Pez Que Fuma was struck dumb. We huddled around the machine, with barely enough room for the three of us, and slowly mumbled in unison as we parsed the unexpected facsimile transmission already fast fading from its waxy roll of faxy paper.

Hog wash, it read, Don't pay any attention to those who would deter you from the course of Reason. You three have a mission, and that mission is the nurture of human freedom (an idea you are, currently, largely ignorant of) in the verity of its cradle-time. Fear not. If you stand firm in your Republican resolve and choose the high road and viaduct of democratic institutions, democratically initiated and democratically promulgated, great honor will adorn your heads in a time to come you cannot imagine, when giant iron statues of the three of you, you Z'huq, and you El Pez Que Fuma, and even you Twin Donuts, shall embellish the Avenue of Liberation, near the Stadium and Bureau of Labor Statistics in a glittering, metropolitan Mitake-Mura you cannot begin to

● 53

imagine. A Mitake-Mura of classical ivy scroll, and fullest amplitude; a Mitake-Mura of uniform Boil, haircut fee; of standard Pepper Percolation and storagable Pipe-Organ, of Rudolph's System of Stops; of Tenebrate Rebaptism, of all sizes of printing type; of boll weevils, flower weevils, cowpea pod weevils; of cockleburr weevils; of ironweed weevils; of zoonomy and zootomy; of skunks *ad judicium*; of triggerfish *imo pectore*; of the wattlebird *qualis ab incepto*; of unaccountable accountability and the crusted accrual of goodwill; of legal accordions and banisters; of Batophobia and the African Goose; a Mitake-Mura of braille, republican cartilage and reflexive placentology; of chock and chaw and the college for the meek and rabbit-eared; of Van Reckinghausen's Illusion and all its crystal knock-offs; of popes and popcorn; of buffer sleeves, windows, elevating knobs, tripods, telephones and telephone wires; of the rangy and rank regardless of rank and rangy; of sensitive plants and singers of noodle; of stereoisomerisms and chambers of deputies, nautiluses, ammonites of ammonia and nitrate; of offices at fabulous tabernaculi; of Romulus and Rhesus and Samuel Adams; of bullet and ballot and cashflow and layoff and downsize and diss and dormer and dignity and deregulate and damage control and the mystical rights of the unborn and the President elect and all those who escape detection on the walls and under the wallpaper of the Senate and under the benches of the House of Representative where the nigger-in-the-woodpile awaits the revivifying word that corporations and not individuals are true persons, as the Supreme Court has decided in *Plessy vs. *Rose* and that dot is dot and redot and the only rose is rose and her name is *Rose.

Fear not.

But fear, we did.

● ● *{How the Start Got Unbegun}:*

And all this time we humble Mitake-Murans had assumed, like the Jackdaw of Rheims, that no one, no one OUT THERE, had any interest in us, or our ways. I cannot convey to you the sense of wonder, the sense of pride we all felt at that moment: the sense that however low and mediocre we were in our private circumscribed existences, that by this accident of destiny, orchestrated by the agency of our fax machine, we suddenly glimpsed, if but for a brief instant, a small patch of the divine woof and warp with the majesty of its system of linked anomalies, each one like a knot in an endless array of fishing net, whatever a "fishing net" might be. So fear gave way, through time, to the saving thought of grace and probable election. Surely we must be a stuff upon which other, nobler stuff is written, surely. And, yea, the little black box of our telepathic connection to both forbears and afterbears continued to rattle on and on, each time enlightening us with observations, critique, useful suggestions concerning our assumptions, mores, fashion crises and the wisdom, logic and relative sensitivity or insensitivity of our hitherto unexamined lingo. We were becoming suave and zipped of lip, like our social betters at both ends of the *Rosean Continuum, our now necessary colleagues and co-incidentals in the criminal saga of time. Time stolen, as it were.

To dot, dot and re-dot. Wowee, it made the head to spin.

Some of us handled this sea-change in our social conditioning better than others. La Pez Que Fuma at least possessed sufficient smarts to grasp the necessity for attempting the reform of our manners, and improvement of our conduct in general. Z'huq, however, soon proved an utter washout at social graces; suffice to say, he was quickly excluded from our soirees and the now regular cotillions we marked, marked with floral levity and much witty chat, the precession of the *Rosean. Z'huq spent all his days hunched over the older, passe faxes, trying to decipher their meanings even when, as was mostly the case, these meanings had long been superseded by newer, more pertinent faxes. For in truth Z'huq

● 55

turned out to be a bit of a grind; this and the lamentable state of his linen caused much mirth among us, La Pez Que Fuma and myself, Monsoor Twin Donuts. We would discuss these and other failings of Z'huq at our weekly sessions of the Frond Society, a charitable group and tax-exempt foundation whose goal it was to give voice and support to the redemption of our less fortunate Mitake-Murans so that they might be better suited to ... to ... whatever state of social whatever the Governors, that is, Monsoor La Pez Que Fuma and myself, Monsoor Twin Donuts, might think best. Ipse dixit.

Z'huq would rush up crowing, there is a logic here. And La Pez Que Fuma and I would lift our aristocratic noses in the approved gesture of contempt, while rolling our eyes in haughty condescension as if to say (which out of politeness we never did): of course, of course, you ninny-hammer, whatever are you driving at? Why proclaim the obvious when it has been obvious from the very first faxes that there is a logic to all this? The existence of such a logic is the fundamental root of Being that all civilization such as we know (or have heard about through the medium of electronic facsimile transmission) is builded. Our little titter through folded fans seemed hardly to ruffle the feathers of that thick-skinned swine, Z'huq. The brute. No, no, no, he blubbered, we have no way of knowing what any of these actually mean— throwing a great mitful of the faxes up into the luminous lemon-lime stratosphere of our little world. Z'huq, the brute. Since each one seems to be a response to another there seems to be no way to assess what any of them really is about, I mean really means for us, here, on Mitake-Mura. Just then the red eye of our Panasonic blinked, and reblinked greenish-white, the color of nickel oxide, the hue of chalcedony, the hue of Mitake-Mura.

Fools, fools, fools, it spoke in the rattle-tongue of thought being written, fools, fools, fools. Not only have you entirely missed the point of the Pretty Times Done Did, but you have let our secret rituals to go unobserved, and allowed dandelions to sprout in the Pyxis of Zeus, Zenobia and Zaphnaphpaneah.

Further you have cross-pollinated the Jacobin and the pigeon producing the Jacobin Pigeon. In a similar fashion you have wrongly conflated the higher concept of box with wood, creating a shrub called boxwood, neither of the tribe of phloem and Xylem, nor suitably boxlike. Should these things come to be mixed up in the mind, the mind itself becomes mixed-up; social discourse shall become a sham of mixed-up hypotheses; should social discourse become such, a mix-up of rinkus and dinkus, why then, society and all that has to do with society shall become a Callithumpian hayride, the affair of fools and landrakes and the whole motley of the unreslanted self-deceived. Beware.

Even within the decorous privacy of our sessions at the Frond Society, La Pez Que Fuma and I, Twin Donuts, were concerned: something about the nature of the faxes had changed; their tone, their tenor, their undertone. Something like a sense of menace could be perceived in the newer ones, not to mention the disturbing and contradictory nature of their respective point of origin, beginning with the instance just cited—some two Yatto-dots plus and minus *Rose, an incomprehensible location in spacetime since it appeared to originate both in the distance past and the distant future.

By now Z'huq pretty much avoided us completely, ostensibly because La Pez Que Fuma and I had declared our Radical Republic without consulting him, and had declared ourselves joint Shed-Masters in perpetuity, thus eliminating our now reviled third wheel from all public duties, posts, privileges and responsibilities. Indeed, we had changed the lock to the shed without informing the poor has-been, so that he only learned of our new dispensation once it had been carried out. Indeed, we could barely contain ourselves at the sight of silly old Z'huq hopelessly sobbing at the threshold of the door to the shed, with all the transmitted facsimiles of felicity it contained, prostrate on the dusty doormat.

But our schemes possessed deeper pockets and longer legs than mere humiliation, for at one of our silences at the Frond Society, La Pez Que Fuma suggested a causal connection

● 57

between the increasingly bizarre tone of the faxes and the nominalist obsessions of our deposed Z'huq. Twin Donuts, he purred, doesn't it seem as if it might, in point of fact, be Z'huq's fault that those High Ones behind the faxes have waxed and waned wolfish and wrathful? His well-established Z'huquian doubt and cynicism regarding the foundation of well-being—surely a matter beyond ratio-linear dubeity—must have registered with the High Masters whence these missives originate. If our Mitake-Muran errors now seem too prolific for political correction do we not all—that is, you and me: La Pez Que Fuma and moi, Mister Twin Donuts—stand in the need of prayer, fasting and perhaps even some propitiative act, possibly live sacrifice or banishment to the outer dark by means of King Saul's mousetrap; and I am not talking dwarf willow talk. I am talking tall turkey. Z'huq, that goose, must pay in the skin to regain our good-standing in the eyes of the fax-masters, whether plus or minus *Rose. That is my idea.

La Pez Que Fuma's eyes glowed like burnished brass on their trembling eyestalks, and his hunched form swayed in the dismal weeds and laces of his antique gowns, now all fantastical ruin, shreds and tangle. Then again I am not much to look at either with my ripped Grateful Dead tee-shirt, and clumsily antiquated orthopedic shoe. Both of us, however, do share a certain nobility of soul; and this constitutes the bond between: an adamant of liberum veto, jouvence blue, and equalibrious jackery.

King Saul's mousetrap, by the way, is an ancient machine resembling a teeter-totter that according to rumor, none of us could recall with whom or where it started, could be used to jettison the unwary, unwanted Mitake-Muran into the abyss of deep space, from the dizzying precipice of our little world's pointy North Pole, a place previously alluded to.

But Z'huq, obviously sensing dimly that a danger loomed in the Mitake-Muran half light, had disappeared. We first searched for him at the narrow place near the Narrow Place, at the North Pole, just by the surreal wreckage of King Saul's Mousetrap, but no, that was the last place he would conceivably have sought out as a refuge; then, fanning out, we proceeded South, hooting and bellowing and beating on conjugate sections of corrugated iron (left over, presumably, from the construction of the shed, in Prehistoric times) with our mighty shoes. We beat on the evil-looking shrubbery at Nightmary Junction—a collision of termite trails—with one of the odd, metallic flyswatters that could be found littering much of the bright, smooth and sooty South Eastern desert, a place where legend has it all the major religions of the Mitake-Muran lineage have spawned: Phobialatry, the blind worship of fear; Buggy-buggy, the worship of gnats; Analumininesciencia, the fearful worship of blindness; and of course, Ultra-faxism, the belief of those like us, La Pez Que Fuma and myself, Twin Donuts, in the divine nature of the precious facsimiles we had been receiving since, well, since we knew not when precisely, as it is against the unfurling unfathomozzle of the *Rose for us to be bothered exactly—but not so long ago.

We searched as best we could. No sign anywhere of Z'huq. Even in the subtropical hell of the South Polar Region, no sign of his Yankee Clipper flip-flop tracing. Only a wilderness of bracken, broken light-bulbs, bangly groves of slime-eating Marquesan pitcher-plants, Sapodilla and the wild Star of Bethlehem. One might succumb to an ague here, a right or left-angled guan ague of Inwit and Agenbite, as was remora'd, long ago by a suction of rumor, wanton weed. So we fled. Of course the one place we knew was safe from Z'huquian transgression was our inner sanctum, the shed. For La Pez Que Fuma, as Master of the Shed, had changed locks during his late term, hadn't he? Of course, neither of us cannot have not, or can we? Recall, Twin Dee, to recall in detail please. Some few dots before the current exfolia of *Rose in her rosy splendor. Ah yes. Only— what?

● 59

● ● ● *{*Rose Reveng'd, or How It All Began Again}:*

Amend all that. La Pez Que Fuma, that dolt, has transmitted to me a thing I am unable to record without dread. Dratful dread. It was his assumption that among my responsibilities during my recent term as Shed Master was the changing of the locks. Because, so he says, in our perfect Radical Republic, all duties and responsibilities are shared, all hierarcheries are abolished so that the face of tyranny be draped in black velour for all time. All epithets retaining to the outcast and reprobate, such as "lowclass", "moronic", "cheesehead" (whatever that is), "brown elbow" and "postmodern academic slimeball" are to be replaced by the new term, *Z'huquian*. Which shall refer to, and encompass a wilderness of erroring mirrors. Such as the charge that is, has somehow fallen upon my shoulders, the broad shoulders of Citizen Twin Donuts, to do what clearly lay within his own job description at that time as Cosmic Shed-Master. Namely, the changing of that damned Yale padlock with another, similar damned Yale padlock, one similar but differently configured in the key department.

Z'huquian fool, La Pez Que Fuma shouted.

Z'huquian loser, I retorted, red faced.

We glare democratically into each other's fierce lemon-drop eyes, eyes angrily bulging forward on their respective eyestalks.

We gather up our tools, baskets of knick-knacks, needles, fiddles, fardels of phlox and Morning Glory, funnels for bimetallic Xanthium, symbolic turnbuckles, and an array of Mirdite false-foliage and other imitations of leaves; we then flash forward intransitively to the primal scene of Ultra-Fax, our humble if rumpledown shed in the shadow of the dead succum tree.

We bang on the door—sure enough it blows open at the first pop of wind up. No one's within, but clearly something is amiss; all about is evidence of Z'huq and things Z'huquian. His slacks and shirt folded neatly over the sleepy cordovan of the easy chair; his hat, a nondescript fez of licorice hue drooped on a rusty nail hammered, sloppily, into the crossbeam over the

60

door aimless doorframe; his eremite's battered suitcase full of crumpled faxes, and notepad after notepad filled with amateurish attempts at exegesis; his wristwatch, a second-hand Dexter Laramie, his talonless bolo, his crushed packet of cheap cheroots, a box of matches from Zax in San Francisco (whatever that is), and a brief note scribbled on half a postcard from "Azure-sanded Linda Susan" in his typically tremulous, spidery hand:

> Dear Pals:
> I am going, going, going, gone. Faxed to a realm beyond your ken, in the transmundane of *Rosetime, a place blessed and twice-blessed for, whatever else it contains, you two (vicious La Pez Que Fuma, rabid Twin Donuts) will not be there. Eat my dust, and grow calluses of envy upon your uncouth pads.
> All best, Z'huq.

For cunning Z'huq has fled by means of fax. He has, apparently, contrived to transmit himself to a far away sub-realm of *Rose, minus or plus. La Pez Que Fuma looked at me, and I looked at him. Each of us convinced of the other's complicity in Z'huq's escape. My hand sought for the unlocked heavy Yale that lay on the table, in the shadow of the door. As La Pez Que Fuma smiles wanly at me, the fax machine once more rattled to life: only... now I see it. Now I see it. This. For the truth is this is the way the world ends. This is the way the world ends not with a cry not with a whimper and those who ride the *rose ride the * ride the * without so much as a smatter of matter, and. Drat, La Pez Que Fuma, there is no more fax paper. There is no more. Z'huq, that fiend, that....[3]

● 61

---

[3] Here ends the mss. of the Matter of Mitake-Mura, much bloodied, torn and chewed about the lower portion of the final page.

What follows is excerpted from the *OICOS OHOLLAH* of Z'huq, a priest and prophet of Eulalia:

● ● ● ● *{clinch}*:

And in my torment I drew myself up into a ball of pure energy and delight; for my enemies had prepared an awful end for me: expulsion into the void by means of an awful engine. My enemies reviled me, and made my every living moment a living hell. I sought them out time after time in an effort to avoid confrontation. All to no avail. My enemies desired only my destruction and would suffer me no saving grace.

And so I myself thought how I would overmaster them, and I drew myself up in the form of a ball of fire. A ball of pure energy and delight. A ball of fur taken from the pelt of the Himalayan snow leopard, certain tufts and wisps of the whiskey-jack along with a portion of myrtle-berry wax. In this form my radiance grew rational and cunning. And I knew these two excitable ne'er-do-wells were riding perilously close to the hot time-wire of the *Rose as it wriggled through the sticky, inert mass of Bobbin's Cheese, which comprises the primal stuff of all subsequent stuff. Pre-stuff, you might call it; proto-stuff. And I knew all I had to do was REMOVE the fax paper from the fax machine, and they would likely go mad; and as I examined the fax machine in the dim light of the single, swaying 60 watt light bulb overhead, I perceived that the roll of paper was nearly used up in any case and I had little trouble wrenching what remained from its spool. And as I hunched over the fax machine, an ingenious idea occurred to me; an ingenious idea that was to be my salvation. And this idea was to transmit MYSELF as electromagnetic energy out of the dismal bondage of Mitake-Mura into the fax machine of whatever other world I might happen, through the Agency of the Unseen, to dial.

And having drawn myself up into a ball of pure delight and energy I dialed and dialed and dialed and dialed and dialed and dialed and dialed until I recognized a welcoming beep of recognition. Out the window I could just barely make out rising puffs of dust as Twin Donuts and La Pez Que Fuma rushed like madmen down the long, solemn declivity of the Mamoodi Highlands, along the Avenue of Nameable Cheeses. I altered my shape a bit so as to be able to fit within the carriage of the machine and rolling myself nearly entirely around the glistening platen, pushed the start button with my last protruding digit, tremblingly. And, as a terrible banging began on the door I was transmitted in a trice—only my soiled Mitake-Muran garments remained.

The rest is history, a thing documented.

I stand, scrolled up before you, glittering in my seven sapphires, runcinates of leaf chicory, Zoathra and tegumenta of Zanzibar gold hammered so thin it trembles—a wellspring of Vision, happiness and the joyful Ohollah.

As for my misfortunate colleagues, all I know of them is little: how, consumed by bigotry and a boundless hatred of all things "Z'huquian", their Radical Republic dissolved into a fearful state of nature, chaos and tin-can banging anarchy. Soon both La Pez Que Fuma and Twin Donuts are accidentally and successively ejected by King Saul's Mousetrap; they mutter endless curses at each other, at the fax machine endlessly chattering far below, at the image of me that obsesses them and against all things as they orbit and re-orbit the mother of all their mysteries, Mitake-Mura, the mother of all the fictitious faxes they shall never, never receive.

MUAZZEZ

◆ *{Bump}:*

They lied to me about the reality of things here on Muazzez. About the foundation of these, their basis, their fundament, the profound bottom of things. I am an Abandoned Cigar Factory (or ACF) groaning in the dunes near the settlement at Culpepper. That alone would be of little interest because there are many abandoned cigar factories near Culpepper. However I am the only one of these many Abandoned Cigar Factories to possess both a telephone booth (nestled handily within the deep recesses of my abandoned tool shed) and also a zygodactyl foot, as of a parrot or vulture.

But they lied to me, when I was a child, small and naïve, and not always able to discern truth from falsehood. Now it is a fact that abandoned cigar factories are, in general, a notoriously gullible bunch; in this regard I am typical of my tribe. But we are also steadfastness incarnate; and surely this steadfastness must be worth something—something more than a brazier's dredge. Our steadfastness has given us abandoned cigar

◆ 65

factories—so far as we know, the sole human inhabitants of the wondrous world of Muazzez—a certain fixed and unchangeable constancy, a resolute loyalty to the deep, dark truths of the unreadable three-legged race of a steam engine that is Muazzez; without this steadfastness, we would be as thistles in the wind (whatever "thistles" are; whatever "wind" is).

Now the story of how I came to be lied to revolves in an... what is the word? The human mind?... like a dead rat in a Simmons Pot. By all accounts, this place, moss-colored Muazzez, ever since the departure of the winged and entitled ones, the High Eulalians I mean, has remained an apolitical postscript. A place whose spindle legs no longer tremble in anticipation of the aroma romantica of the noble ...y... cigar. Of the Eulalians themselves nothing, I presume, is known since if something were to be known surely I would know it, or its rumor at least. All things knowable do possess their attendant rumors, skipping and snapping happily at the heels of whoever the thing known amounts to, and is. But the drift of this thought is not my drift, for there is no drift to my thought. My thought is a rooted thing.

My nearest neighbor, an abandoned cigar factory by the name of Finn, resides there, on the other side of the heavenly ditch known only as Becquerel's Radiant, and is my main man and source of useful information regarding the ways of the world, and its twirl; the ways of the world of Muazzez. Finn has assured me in his deep, deep booming that what most characterizes our world in its primeval yerk and jerk is a primal radial symmetry, as of a series of spokes or spokey type spindles radiating from a deep and frosty central secret; a secret which is in the habit of sitting in the middle, while the rest of us hunch up or hunker down, equally remote, and endure our eternal ignorance seated on the wide circumference of what we all suppose. What we wrongly choose to suppose. Clearly, Finn's rabbit ears are more finely attuned than my tin ones, which on the gradient of things are but a tincal (*tinqkal*) to his fine talcum, tincal being only a crude, unsophisticated borax of Malayan extraction. So I am careful to listen, careful to hear what my wise neighbor tells me regarding the deep, deep things. Finn passes on to me what Finn has heard before, and this is called civilization. Now the immediate problem is, I do not know how to pass on what I know, as there is no man (permit me this humble euphemism) beyond me, noman, nemo; there is none to whom I might in my booming, impart and export the import of my chilly Muazzezian doom. There is simply no room for doom on this part of the world; that is, beyond some tinkers and Bong Farmers (people without souls) from the titration plants over in Hillsbrother, near the mound of coffee grounds, matchless mounds it should be noted, a topless tower of a mound comparable in airy amplitude to me, or to Finn. Tinkers lost in a tinker's dream that is only an homage to some cosmic Titivillus, lesser god of misprints and perennial fly in the ointment of the Cosmic Text. No more about these, however, and the hideous refrigerator cartons they have a way of setting up near the Pharoanic mass of us; each and every one of us more massy and Pharoanic than the last; all persisting in time's graceful and gradual phase-out beneath the inky skies of moss-colored Muazzez; Muazzez, the only world of all the small worlds (could there be, truly, more small worlds than this?) that has been deserted not only by the High Eulalians but also by the higher concept of tennis. But the higher concept of tennis, tennis with her tendency to bounce, bounce and so on, and thus to elude us, and to escape easy grasp, belongs not to One (Bump) nor to Two (Tilt) but to Three (Laugh it Off). And owing to our pursuit of deep, deep truths—final things, Finn would say—; not to mention our longstanding policy of steadfastness; we have not yet arrived at that third place, that puzzling place of grammatical impasse.

Bumps are another sort of impasse; bumps are the habit of proceeding by jerks and jolts, or by yerk and jerk as is the case on Muazzez where there is no weather, but of a cold so cold it is a frozen bull-roarer and of heat so hot it is of the tribe of bunsen burner; bumps *qua* bumps are bumps. Lumps are often hidden beneath the surface of bumpy things and this is especially true of lumpish, imperfect places like this one, a roundy approximately oblong place resembling, I would suppose, no other. Within my fallen walls and carding tables, my long dank rooms where heaped sheaves of moist Havana hung out to dry, I recollect in aromatic tranquility under the rusted swaying sign of ...y...

Still I differ from all other abandoned cigar factories in one respect, one key respect, at least one, one germane to the Muazzezian narration here deployed. I am referring to my zygodactyl claw which has enabled me to do a little subterranean exploration on my own. I cannot believe any other of the abandoned cigar factories of Muazzez incorporate this useful feature. Even Finn, to whose absolute mastery in matters magisterial and in the molding dish of superior wisdom, I bow or rather lean, is lacking in this respect. As bumps occur, I am able to partially alleviate the force of their impact. Where the bumps come from is beyond mortal reason, that net beyond which lies the realm of what noise, what alien racket, and beyond that and beyond that and beyond that a baseline regressing shot by shot into an infinity even the High Eulalians in the dawn of time knew not the extent, neither by their cunning craft of measuring worm, nor by leap of light's hare, nor by the malign craft of Time's inky wormhole. Bumps are bumps I reckon, and my claw has digged a little deeper during each of them, clutched at each random impact deep down into the fateful stuff of Muazzez, till at long last I begin to perceive a cunning arrangement of layers. I perceive an order in the fundament, just as Finn has asseverated. The more deeply down one delves, Finn declared, the more repetition becomes the rule of the day; the more heavy, inorganic and deeply serious all matters become. The rule of radial symmetry rules all wisdom, even on lumpish, moss-colored Muazzez. As I dig and scratch, scratch blindly and clumsily, as if impelled by a force more basic than mere bumpness, I become convinced like the great geometer Pascal that the riddle of the world's runic confusion resides experientially and experimentally contrived in a vertical grammar only the happy few are capable of deciphering. Happy in my fewness, and in the sparseness of my delight, I would have genuflected to myself, or at least bowed before my image floating like Narcissus on the oily rain-water of Becquerel's Radiant had I not been wary of some structural overstrain in my supporting timbers, long out of service and subject to sprain, rot or worse. It is lonely to be so alone in wonderment; indeed, to be so alone in the wonderment of full knowledge often feels like being alone in the empty cigar box (of course, an ...y... box) of bafflement and ignorance. Total things are radically hinged to the same hub and the same spindly spokes connect grace, purpose, triumph and luck to their opposites both in gravity and degree. Radical symmetry revolves around a mare's nest of darkest centralia, deep and profound.

For instance, in the Marginate Sphere of Bump I encountered first plain old gypsum, then in succession ruddy pangolinite, spongy Uriah stuff, wriggle of lead, and finally pentacle of Ytterbium. In the more rarefied Marinara system I initially scraped and tore through layers of Make Out, Make Shift, Make Ready, only to reach my horny uttermost at a skimpy deposit of Make Mountain out of a Mole-Hill. On the Market Value Sliding Scale System (founded by our nameless predecessors, even before the Eulalians—I am talking about the god-like beings who actually designed and builded the cigar factories—bodies without souls in that void, inenerrable era.) I carefully take note of the following more or less clearly defined substratums: Empathy, Embrangle, Emote, Embowel, and lastly Emission of Admission. Up to this point, regularity and the uniformitarian hypothesis seem to work out much as Finn had indicated it would. Knowledge lay heaped up, like a heap of bottle caps or cigar bands—and the sky? the sky larked about in her mystic absence, larked this way and that, as though dodging the massive fist of sudden infant child death syndrome. All about me lay tri-square, according to Vervier's Law.

♦ ♦ *{Tilt}*:

I hope you can follow my drift, for try as I might it is almost always elusive to me even though I am present in much of it. Drifts about the self, especially complex and highly evolved selves, selves like abandoned cigar factories, have a way of sliding off into places beyond the beaten path, places like non-self hedges and the hegemony of the self's perfect picture of the world and all things in it. In the best of all possible worlds that perfect picture comes to replace the self, which is a messy, nasty and vile set of arbitrary constructions at best. However, standing as I do, at the very apex of the stepladder of creation, I do not need such a stratagem, as my energies are always perfectly focussed upon their object. Steadfastness, you will recall. But the nightmare alterity of steadfastness is likewise rooted to the same hub; for stead-fastness and all her children like the house of stone are also on *sand ybuilded*. That is why bumps of all shapes are drawn to steadfastness as snakes are to sugar-beans, and bears are to honey (what's a "bear"? and what is a "honey"?).

Precept: Bumps are drawn to what is bumpable.

Bumps are drawn to that which is bumpable, and the most bumpable of all objects are those which are mostly steadfast; for those which are most steadfast invariably are the most invariant. I must say if I were a bump I would search high and low for an object of utmost steadfastness to bump upon, because such an object constitutes an ideal target in that regard, as it allows the approaching bump ample time to locate the object squarely in its cross-hairs, and to stamp and clear away all behind and to heighten one's intensity by anticipation of the imag-ined impact with the steadfast one who for her part reciprocates by not stooping to the low, but all too common resort of the unsteadfast; namely, dodging, ducking, stepping aside or attempting otherwise to frustrate the onrushing bump, now engorged with the pure delight of inescapable collision. But then I don't care for bumps very much. I do not much care for the way they comb their hair. And although I sometimes think it would be a delight, just for once, to get down off my mound of crumbing foundation stones (I surmise those are stones down there) and haul my ruinous ponderation up to the top of a hill, like Mt Sizable Artichoke, there across the far wriggle of Becquerel's Radiant as it disappears over Finn's shoulder across the Great Nguba (Goober) Plain; from whence I would come roaring down upon an unsuspecting campsite of off-season Bumps, Bumps with their wives and children and clotheslines and licorice salad, and give them a taste of their own medicine. Wouldn't that be an unforgettable sight: me, twelve acres of crumbling brick and mortar, thousands of tons of abandoned cigar factory, emerging in full glory out of the elms and sycamores, crested by vines and garlands of blueberry and rosebush; glaring with intense, almost infernal, malevolence before the final, awful, thunderous charge down, down, down upon the squealing bumps below. Still, I know this urge is a low one; it is an impulse that our kind have long ago transcended. But the truth is, bumps even of the lowliest kind, like the bumps accidentally incurred by the tinkers and Bong farmers in their sad drunken revels, are to be taken seriously. For even the most steadfast of the steadfast has somewhere a crack, however faint, flowing waywardly up its massive foundation stone, and a crack, any crack, is a fatal flaw in the steadfast. From cracks flow faults, and from these all manner of dialectical materialism. Bumps lead to tilt, as of the Pisan hypotenuse, and tilt issues forth normally into topple and topple is the lead cause of stop and what stop initiates is as inevitable as the fact that, according to the International System of the Academy of Sciences, the SI unit for inductance is Henry (symbol: H); namely, full stop. Full stop, period. Beyond that terminus no man can go, even if like me, she is an abandoned cigar factory. And what undergirds all this ambulatory frightwig of unappetizing complication is the immootable problem of what prompted all that Radial Symmetry in the first place. Because what this might be can only be, at bottom, a bump, a bump in the night. Finn, I have noticed, never dwells on these topics, at least in any detail.

♦ 71

Indeed, Finn does not retail in detail because as the saying goes, God is there (whoever God is) and the spider also.

There, I think I have covered Bump, although again Finn would say I have not done so. In truth Finn would have a puntilla in the regard that in covering bumps I had not covered him, and from a certain disinterested prospect it might just be possible to regard Finn and all his Finnish friends (Tribe of Suomi?), myself among them, all the wild dispersion of abandoned cigar factories near Culpepper and beyond, as a mere bunch of bumps, outsized bumps to be sure, but bumps nevertheless. Bumps, further, disguised bumpishly as ACFs and so totally lacking in ethnic authenticity. Deracinated lumps of bump, trembling in age-old terror beneath a cloth of disguise so habitual it no longer registers as cloth. An unseen mesh or screen, as of the sort the Higher Eulalians would employ to trap fat bumblebees for their feast on Luna, and Bang. Worlds lost to history through the primal loss of the radial symmetry that starts up where the previous start stopped.

Indeed, can one ever be said to have covered Bump? Because a covered bump turns into a lump, and we are back where we began. And this cycle of arid hunches has no further extension in thought, or in the heart's nomenclature, only in the infinite interstices of time. I shudder to think. And so, I do not; instead, I stop.

And so, as I was saying, they lied to me about the profound bottom of things here on Muazzez. But you believe all things when you are small, even when you are a mere lewis (a dovetailed iron tenon made of several parts and designed to fit into a dovetail mortise in a large stone so that it can be lifted by a hoisting apparatus), a mere twinkle that is, in the eye of a sheet bend (a knot in which one rope or piece of yarn is made fast to the bight of another). Now, who did the telling, that I do not know, that I cannot say. It is a mystery, much like the one I mentioned earlier, the problem of not knowing how, precisely, to pass on what I know. Each end of life's road is blocked by a long-handled rake lying dangerous and emblematic, teeth up, across the path destiny seems to have chosen for me. If I proceed with my clumsy lack of feet, my undextrous lower portions rumbling along at their centipede pace; the long hardwood handle of which rake, upon the depression of the row of teeth by my foundation, flies up invariably, and whacks me hard upon the window or doorway of my face. And this consequence follows, follows whether or not I proceed cautiously forward or cautiously back; or incautiously forward or incautiously back. Bear in mind there is scant difference—the merest scintilla of measurable velocity difference between my most rapid progress and my least—so that this variation does not count for much in the matter. In either direction I face an insuperable terminus, and so must rely upon whatever I can glean from my neighbor, Finn. The cycle runs something like this: Finn knows and, possessing no claw, speaks; I listen to what Finn says and think I know, only doubts creep in, and I know that I do not know, I am faking it; besides, there is no one around for me to pass on what I know, what Finn has told me, so I have to sit quietly minding my own business (a thing anathema to human nature); so I grow bored and begin to tap my foot; in this way I discover I possess a foot—I simply did not know before; experimenting with my foot (I possess only one) I begin to move it around a little, this way and that, and come to the realization that this foot is shaped like a crow's foot, or talon; this appendage, I soon discover, is capable of digging, ergo I begin to dig (was it the geometer Pascal who said, when a hammer is the only tool you possess everything begins to look like a nail?); by digging, I discover the joys and wonders of excavation, and thereby come partially to discover my own nature, if an abandoned cigar factory may be said to possess a nature, a nature beyond the obvious.

And if the matter ended there, fine.

And if the matter ended there, one could say the matter ended there, and be done with it. And if the matter ended one could say life on Muazzez resembles that of any normal world, any normal small world (is it not in the nature of a world to be a small world?), endlessly and comfortably repeating the egg and dart motif along a cloudless Muazzezian sky of ever unscrolling ornamental frieze? One could say that, I suppose.

And if the matter ended there I would have no complaint, as there would be nothing radically amiss to complain about, except for the question of a few idle details. Let us not go into the matter of that right now because, as I have mentioned before, Finn does not retail in detail and also God lives there, and the spider too. And I have a horror of both.

But logic is a terrible machine and no one can stay its witless, participial tamboura, tamboura, tamboura. Even on Muazzez, a place I now realize to be a merely accessory being, of no particular importance in the greater, or lesser, or whatever scheme of things. Like a smoke. Smoke, smoke from a time that has passed into memory, and from memory into imagination, and from that into some chronicle of the madness of small worlds.

As I have reported, Muazzez is of the color of moss, or sassy-hued schist and flinkite with flakes of emerald smagdarine. Not terribly attractive, unless the sun, or whatever it is, lies just below the lip of the horizon when you can see refracted—the green light pouring through the stony fibers as though these were living filiamentia—the delicatest nerves of some living things. And the sky of Muazzez, when not obliterated by the dark black of night, attains at noon something of the indescribable hue of a lemon blossom, just as it has unfolded from its bud; or as the sap of the lime, mixed with the juice of the tamarind. And I mention these because, on such occasions there is a sweetness to the air that cuts through even the pungent regret of my dark, nicotine-stained walls; something about such scents that can almost reduce me to tears, though what part of me might be capable of such a powerful sentiment I would not venture to imagine. But everybody knows that old theaters are haunted, so I would not be surprised if there may be spirits lodged deep within my walls, and down under the heavy timbers that crisscross the colossal nave of my interior structure, extending clear from sorting rooms (narthex) to the chancel of my counting room, with deep aisles where patient *trabajadores* sat at desks, rolling patiently my finest Havana while at his pulpit far above, the lector solemnly read from his Cervantes and Shakespeare and Babunin. Peace reigned in the worker's hearts because all knew that each tenth cigar would be his or her own.

But the matter did not end there.

But the matter could not possibly have ended there because, both in visual expanse and vertical drop, the matter seemed endless, or of an extent of some cubic miles at least. The exact nature of this layering, for layering there clearly was, came both to perplex and finally obsess me. Before too long I had dug my way deep into a hole of investigatory Boogie Woogie. I became overwhelmed by the force of pure curiosity, as if my single thought were to will one thing. To ding some subterranean bell. I sought to examine what lay below, and delve into the issue of the Chthonic. And so I did, all forty-two layers, some more memorable than the rest; a confection whose pure decorative perfection, for a time, took the cake and handed it to me on a silver pladder. Mere utility I despised. The bright core of Radical Symmetry summoned and I knew my mission was to probe that place and reveal what lay there, be it boot or booster cable. To hell with bumps, and all things bumpy; I would go in search of myself, following the pure plumb line of my will, and follow where it led, even to the Koresh hollow of Muazzez's deepest plumbing.

And so, in succession a stratigraphic variorum. First, *bonnyclabber*, the layer of sour, clotted cream; then *brocade*, the candlewax of certain sacred places, places devoted to the placing of jars and the jarring of places, many of them from Cipangu (wherever that is); *bursitis*, a lovely inflammation extending throughout Muazzez's bursa, as it does in the shoulder, tennis elbow (whatever "tennis" is) or knee; *charcoal rot*, an unpleasant stratum, foul and decayed; *a layer composed entirely of clucks and tympanous clucking*, as of a person calling a horse; cold cuts, also known as the sandwich layer; *concertina*, a smallish instrument with bellows and buttons—its

♦ 75

muffled music may be heard at the bottoms of certain muffled wells; *crème de menthe*, a sticky greenish layer of mint, considered an aphrodisiac among our ignorant tinkers and Bong Farmers; *decrescendo*, a region of decreasing volume; *demijohn*, an expanse of colored glass supported by an odd wicker thatch; *demisemiquaver*, a thirty-second note pressed like a leaf in the middle of all this; *diffraction grating*, a hunk of glass or metal having a large number or very fine parallel grooves or slits in the surface and used to produce optical spectra by diffraction or reflected light; *dreck*, a thin layer of dung; *ding*, a thick layer of druck; *dry as dust*, a collection of postmodern critical theory, mashed and compressed to form a thin, flat (inedible) flatbread; *ejaculate*, a squirt of stuff forcefully expelled; *enflurance*, a nonexplosive anaesthetic, $C_3H_2CIF_5O$; espresso, a sludge residue of Espy, the habit of spying upon, a glimpsing or catching sight of Germans; *face down*, to overcome or prevail by a stare or resolute manner; *freaky*, a layer of that which freaks; *hafnium*, a brilliant, silvery metallic element separated from ores of zirconium, and used in nuclear control rods (what's "control"?); *homespun*, a plain, coarse, woolen cloth made of homespun yarn; *integration*, an organization of organic, psychological and social traits and tendencies of a person into a harmonious, if spotty, whole; *loco foco*, a member of a radical faction of the New York Democratic Party, organized in 1835, long missing and presumed dead; *neverneverland*, an imaginary place where all is idyllic or ideal; *new criticism*, a layer of literary criticism that stresses close reading and posits that the facts of an author's life are irrelevant; *paranoia*, a region of non-degenerative, limited psychosis, typified by delusions of persecution; parasol, a region of small, light umbrellas; *prosopeia*, various impersonations of absent or imaginary speakers; *roman fleuve*, a long novel in many volumes, mostly flattened; *ruff*, a region of stiffly starched frilled or pleated circular collars of lace, muslin, or other fine fabric, worn by men and women in the 16th and 17th centuries; *scene stealer*, a layer composed of actors who are given to the fine art of drawing attention to oneself when one is not meant to be the focus of attention;

Shick test, an intracutaneous skin test of susceptibility to Diphtheria; *Schiff's Reagent*, an aqueous layer of solution of rosalind and sulphurous acid used to test for the presence of aldehydes and jeckylhydes; *shin-plaster*, paper currency issued privately, and devalued by inflation or lack of backing; *simple closed curve*, a region of Jordan curves; *spackle*, a powder stratum, which when mixed with water is used to fill holes in plaster before painting or papering; *squirting cucumber*, a region of hairy vines; *Ecballium elaterium*, having fruit that when ripe discharges its seeds and juices explosively; *stretch receptor*, a proprioceptor in a muscle or tendon that is stimulated by a stretch; *umpteen*, a stratum of large but indefinite numbers; *Umbrella Bird Land*, a wide layer noted for its pop-ulation of several tropical American birds; *Cephaloptereus Ornatus*, hav-ing a retractile black crest and a long, feathered wattle; *vernacular*, a deep stratum of non-standard or substandard speech; upon which I was forced to suspend my excavation owing to what I first perceived, or rather misperceived as a particularly violent bump. The strain of my digging had evidently cleared away a whole mess of underground debris, so much in fact, that tinkers and Bong Farmers from miles and miles around came with their sledges, flatbeds and dumptrucks to haul away the diverse material I had dug and cleared away behind me, mak-ing—predictably—all there a desolation. Even so, the mountain of debris remains to this day a tribute to my folly, Mount Ivy League I named it, because of the fact there were leagues of the stuff, all jumbled together, and because after a few months the prettiest honeysuckle and climbing ivy began to appear, as if by magic, on the attractive, peren-nially sunlit and positively Floridian, south-east slope. What I did not realize was that in clearing away a great deal of the inner Muazzez, I had inadvertently created a great hole, or vacuum, far below, beneath not only the whole Culpeppper region, but beneath me as well, the tons and tons of my longstanding steadfastness. Now, a hole under the right circumstance becomes, for all practical purposes, a vacuum. And we all know from our high school French that a vacuum is something that nature abhoreth.

That bump, which took me so by surprise, was, you see, no ordinary bump; that bump was a tilt, a full tilt, disguised as a bump. How do I know this? Because shortly thereafter I began to hear bits of song, snatches as of angels singing, and crows and toucans. High-pitched and low-pitched shrills, cries and caws, apparently from the deep interior regions of my fundament. But it is impossible with such cries to discover precisely their origin, just as it is often very easy to mistake a cry of passion and fulfillment with one of futility and hitherto untapped sorrow and regret. The deep emotion of these noises somehow charmed and moved me, moved me in that way an unknown music does, fanning out wide over the dreaming face of a lake in the early evening, shrouded by mists as the willows and Spanish moss, damp with dew, hang low in the waning twilight.

At one point one of the voices I had grown accustomed to suddenly modulated unexpectedly into a strange unhuman creak, as of wooden timbers being twisted and their woody fiber creaking under an intense strain. The whole realm of the unhuman poured into the gap between previous expectation and present realization.

Something about this uncanny transformation penetrated deep into my consciousness, and with it a sudden illumination. The assumption I had made about my own humanity now felt as false and fatuous as that of the tinkers and Bong Farmers, peoples I had despised and dismissed. What had I overlooked, to be so entirely off the mark? How could I have so entirely misjudged the matter, so that what I had taken for bedrock now seemed sand, or a porous linearization of some talus or heap of slag? But consciousness is double, and how great a mystery to each of us is our own special, inner architecture! But I have always had faith, for I know one day the telephone in my booth will ring, and at that ringing I will rejoice, for I know that that ringing will be a sign, and whatever that sign stands for there will be joy and glad tidings for all; since I am contained in what we refer to when we denominate a group of entities, all; that I shall likewise share in the common celebration; this even though I am unable for obvious reasons to actually answer the phone in the phone-booth that is lodged deep within me. Indeed, were I able somehow through some mechanical Rube Goldberg device to delicately lift the receiver from off the armature where it resides and raise the instrument to the tympanums of my hallways and doorways, and of my ceilings and floorboards, I should not be able to understand what the voice of the other end was saying; and this even if that voice was speaking in a language I could understand, High School French, for instance. I know this in my heart, and even if I am somewhat abashed in the realization I know facts are facts and to suppose otherwise would only amount to a futile exercise in self-delusion. So the ringing of my inner telephone reminds me of the notion of transcendence, just as the creaking of my timbers and floorboards reminds me of the contingent state of human nature itself, at best a double thing possessed of contrary elements forever locked, as mortise and tenon are, in a union that is both perilous and precarious. Even the human face, which we take for granted on the fronts of houses, on the siding of storage bins and warehouses, in the swaying treetops and cumulo-nimbus, even at the bottom of bodies of water, like Lake Tisane over by Rorschach, are but as a meaningless tussle of breezes, idle commotion signifying mere shilly-shally, signification beyond sign-post.

♦ ♦ ♦ *{Laugh it Off}:*

My world and everything within it is formed of pictures; pictures overlapping other pictures, pictures within pictures, pictures simple. I dreamed once that at the end of my foot was not a claw, but an eye. That I see through, at the very tip of my savage appendage. And do all my dreams take place while I am asleep? Who can tell?

But whether asleep or not I know that when I speak, as now, what I am describing primarily is a picture, although what is to be done with this picture, or any of the ones I have pictured here, is far from clear. Of what use are they? Laugh it off, you say; but I cannot laugh it off, for the picture seems to spare us both labor and its cold reversal, levity. It already points to a particular use. This is how it takes us in.

In any event, I notice my entire edifice has begun to tilt, and I begin to swim in the sandy dunes where I had thought to remain perched forever, forever impregnable in my steadfastness. I have begun to sink into the quartz-stuccoed, cavernous interior I have myself dug. The geode of my own strange folly. As I tilt more I begin to break apart and become severally voiced. Olden times speak through my riven hulk. My right triangle topples over so slowly to an irritating Isocelean incline. Between my toes—whose toes are we discussing, my dear?—a long growing filament; I give it a strong tug, and lean over even more precipitously as the banshee voices of my useless, outmoded architecture whine and shriek; whining and wailing what presage? What multivariate termination? As I draw out the single strand and pull, pull, pull, I discover by microscopic examination that it is one long human hair, and I am drawing myself down, inexorably down toward a quicksand vortex where I shall become embalmed forever within the ruby geode of my own excavation. Deep within Muazzez, the redeeming repetition I so much strove to uncover has failed to appear, for at its very core, curled up so tightly, is only hair. A single strand of hair. So tightly wound up one could bat the whole world, the whole small, mad world of Muazzez, like a tennis ball. Face facts, I boom as the quicksand swallows me whole, clear up to my rusty clanking sign, ...y....

Muazzez is a world of hair.

SAWYER HOGG

● {*SPEED talks SLOW*}:

Fern would not have known how to say it without my help; Fern was slow, and I, her beloved, was fast. How long had we lain in hiding, by the cutback in the canebrake on the blasted slopes of Mount General Rumor, an allegorical and rancid place. Fern was lissome and low; I was lank and long, and together we were lissome and lank. And low, both low. Our embraces involved us in postures so extreme they caused one to doubt the natural order. At times we seemed a Klein Bottle in full transparency, unable to sort out which was whose and how we interacted. Fern fell and took me happily to that place; that was the way I reasoned about the affair later when I had come to my senses, and come out of my senses (not to mention her senses) at the same time. This was the first branching, and given the history of the place, Sawyer Hogg, I do suppose we did so only after taking a vote on the topic. We awoke from the primordial passion of our joined and joint ecstacy, created selfishly in that moment (but democratically so) and enacted the plebescite of separation.

● 83

I never doubted this was the right path to pick because it seemed the right one at the time, and there were only two: To do, or not to do so. To not do so implied a step back somehow, a kind of amorous undoing unbecoming to those, a Klein Bottle duo of the lank and lissome, whose first coming had only just now gathered enough steam to crack the nut, so to speak, of both peak experience and split pea of the mystical and soupy. Life, the moist. For Fern and I subsequently agreed that moist of our life before had been a dry and dim-watted affair; a meager business of Jerusalem lemons, uphill kickback management, long-in-the-tooth staircase winding, pro forma confession and summarizing hikes and hitch-hikes. And narrow escapes from low flying kites and moon-hitches; all the endless tallying and sorting attendant upon life as it was and is on violet-skyed Sawyer Hogg, realm of list voting, plebiscites, proportional representation and all the rest of it. A world of perpetual referenda. Fern had only branched off from the others of her kind (and also mine it must be granted), though an anomaly so intricately interinvolved its necessity could never be unloaded from any ballot box, and counted.

That was the first awakening for me: what shone deep in those delicate dark and violet eyes, what trembled in our clutched hands, somehow eluded all numeration and, fast upon that (for I am not called Speed for nothing), there might contain a bug in the ointment, democratically speaking.

Was that the beginning of, also, of our doom? I wonder now, just as I wondered then even though I was not in a position to decide the issue at that point, obviously. Obviously because I had not polled myself and those others who might feel they had a stake, and therefore felt it was their right to put in their two cents. For we on Sawyer Hogg are a democratic people, with a long tradition of democratic behavior, a tradition that goes back two or three weeks at least, till it be swallowed in the mists of time and prehistory. And for us prehistory is a jambalaya of judgmental non-judgment when we could not hammer out the basis of an agreement concerning anything. But now I have sped beyond myself and must wait for the slow, unadventurous part of me, my unSawyer Hodgian vestigial precipitate, to catch up. Oh, but my sweet Fern, Fern of my dreams, Fern of my passion, how your presence has touched this moonish, wide-eyed face of mine! How your delicate coiled tresses drive me to tell my love, coiled tresses trembling like a coppery mountain brook tumbling down the unimpeachable whiteness of your neck and shoulders. Trembling in sublime negligence! And I know I meant no slander to your sisters-in-citizenship to say none could compare with you, in grace, in grave and serious nonsensical palaver, in hop skip and jump up and down the magnificent slopes of Mount General Rumor, the highest and most mighty of our mountains. But it must be said there were moments when the picture did not appear so rosy and red-headed. This happened all because of a change in the weather, at one of our frequent open-air conclaves we summon to decide all our pressing issues.

Professional politicians we have long regarded as greasy slime, if not potential Bonapartes waiting to reoccur; accordingly we have made a habit of deciding all issues subject to dispute among ourselves, strict-ly. All means truly the utmost of all in this regard, as the issue of the phrase "all issues subject to dispute" might seem a trifle hyper-extend-ed for those not quite so given to the precepts of the genius of liberty. For not only do we decide matters pertaining to taxation and general governance in this fashion, but also conditions such as right or wrong in arguments over the lay of the land, the truth of scientific and philo-sophical propositions, dicta and conundra. We decide also all disputes over the coming and going of the seasons (such as they are on squat, square, spare, poker-faced Sawyer Hogg), even down to the appar-ently random pointillia of the weather itself. No thing escapes opinion on our planet, and you had better believe it because our motto is, we are each and everyone just as good as you and if you don't like it, buster, you can just go and take a hike, because that's the way it is, because that's the way we like it.

Fern, as I was saying, sweet Fern. For she was the sweet elective affinity in the ointment, and my amorous artificer. She made me run, run, run for it. And so I encountered my nature, which hitherto had from me fled. This is what she did without knowing, and I know this for a fact because if she had in sooth known she would have consulted (as I had, humbly, and in full knowledge of grace, probability and statistics) her social betters who would have put the measure to a vote in the provincial legislature. This of course was earlier than the floral jactation of our love; this was in sociology (or was it philosophy?) class in Messy Church Villa where we sat across the aisle as a professor droned and uhmmed, droned and uhmmed the way they do in those parts where rank elitism had flourished until only a little time ago (how little subject to some disagreement, and hence put to a vote as a popular referendum which decided that particular "how little" came to exactly five years, five months and fifteen days, a decision that more than a few (a full majority, in fact) have long regarded as a high point in the history of our proud people. How long exactly have they done so? Let us pass over that for a moment, as a prospect of infinite regress passes before and behind us, like our image (Fern's and mine presumably), folds into its nested antitype in an infinity of folding mirrors, creating an unparallelable problem for those, like myself, who are fully invested in the making of lists and columns; in short, of those who count.

Yes, Fern looked askance and her look bent both time and light till it curled back at me. I felt her glance at the back of my head before I saw it, and what it asked struck with full force. Half her eye hid under the brim of her fabulous lavender hat, a lavender out of time, as we both recalled in amorous unanimity. For such moments cross times in ways that skirt the issue of the better class of pure calculation. As that look did its work of asking I felt the "I" part of me sucked out of my living presence, out the door, out the window, out the keyhole and over the transom and out into the tilted jumble of swallow-swept fields, fields full of light bursting down and far off storms in full dialogue, and a scattering of black and white cows trying to decide whether to stand up or sit down. All this counted clearly, but the ramifications

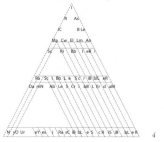

defied consciousneth.

Returning to the room I noticed part of her blouse untucked to reveal an oval of white waist that ruined me. Still her eyes under the brim lowered, as if curtained by her lovely lashes, left a doubt.

Professor Moebius (his very name an incitement to normal melancholy) droned and uhmmed, but even that failed to matter. For time had stopped and stood motionless at a place I had not known before: a place where no shadow fell to pursue Speedo in his flight; a place, if I were able, I would denominate only as one, as one only. One. One, one, one!

In subsequent days we (we in the sense of my assembled countrymen, women and me) would refer to this touching scene as the Miracle at Messy Church, and its fragrance grew legendary among us—Fern alone demurred, claiming exemption from the communally-sanctioned and therefore common rapture on the grounds that her special place in the social construction of the moment did not really afford much of a confirmation of rapturous significance; indeed, her cap was pulled low over her face that day, she confessed when pressed on the point at subcommittee meeting, in order that some nasty scratches might not show; scratches incurred while stealing currants and blackberries that morning out on the lush fields of nearby Fetlock Fairway, with some of her girlish classmates; and that this was

---

[4] a picture of the ramifications

the true cause of her fetching demeanor on that occasion.

Do we ever know what we do?

Do we ever fully know the consequences of what we do? and the potential implication of those actions in the turmoil of the actual as its myriad aspects radiate out, like spokes from the hub of a broken wheel, as the intent accomplishes its corpse through the agency of the lesser gods of Sawyer Hodgian democracy—Rumor, Report and Divine Gossip? For what can be known can be misknown as well, and who can say which is more valuable for the maintenance of Public Health and Public Safety? As with the rifle report that echoes off the far cliff and may even cause the ice to crack and fall catastrophically, so the auditory reception of news from over the hedge and around the narrow pass through to the neighboring gorges (St John's Wrinkle, in this case; a proverbial frog hollow and salient feature of the spectacular Northern highlands of Mount General Rumor) to occasion what outcry, what adulation, what avalanche of mimicry and mischief, what witty new phrase, like wow, man or what furious attachment to a new and special twisted cross; one, too, whose message being buried in a necessary concealment calls out to avenge an ancient crime with an act that balances the equation, so to speak, of luminous doing with the smutch of misdeed. Still Fern the girl was my girl wine and well she knew how well to measure and to pour. Falernian wine of love we know and keep for our own sweet delectation within our private Klein Bottle, love's amphora, as of eld. Fern wine that fills all who remember the Miracle at Messy Church and the number of that moment, as time closes around it, like a wounded sparrow in a deeply caring hand.

But soon after I had won her love and Fern had won mine, cruel fate, intervened, in the form of a special bill duly passed in a joint session of Congress. This special bill was a cumbrous and mammoth affair containing a multitude of disrelated items. To wit: a value-added tax upon street hawkers hawking other than strict necessities on the National Day; prohibition of public art funded through the department of Cultural Affairs which has not been licensed by the Community Board in question; revocation of the license and legal authorization to Rabbis who had not received the prescribed DNA testing to check for inappropriate genetic material; a guide to the rehabilitation and renovation of some 150 superfund sites so that all bidders be made aware of the several distinct types and degrees of toxicity, and the penalties to be incurred by mishmash, mishandling and general bungling; the striking of a special coin at the Franklin mint in the form of a comet on the 19th of May Year Three (a time so remote as to beggar the usual honorifics); a sterilization decree for the Mohan Wrestler, a vulgar brute found guilty of a great number of crimes against public decency, and an alleged disrespector of our late democratic reforms; a resolution to honor the late ambassador to Mexico; another to eliminate the Widows and Orphans Fund, and to reallocate the monies freed up thereby as loans to venture capitalists and casino owners in various states, principalities, reservations and in the Holy City itself (at his Eminence's pleasure); and, lastly, to increase the annual subsidies to farmers of tobacco, toboggans, jute and linen, sheaves and hail, four-crested inkhorns, mothpeas, cotton-tipped wolfberries, wagonweed, beets, crow fodder, mute onions, soya, instant coffee, horse tails, rabbit ear celery and hog-belly futures. Snuggled somewhere in all this mass of detailed and exquisitely crafted legislation was the apparently insignificant item:

> 23-6(b). The person known as and henceforth referred to as FERN X, of _____ Minwalla Road, in the county of Sleaziks, is to be gender-reversed on the 22nd of August, this year, as part of this legislation under the Civil Trust Act (Civil Code, Volume 18, Section 401, paragraph G.3.a.).

Thunderstruck, I sat down hard and hurt myself in a way that ought not to be discussed without a special permit, a permit known as the Permit of Perhaps because it is quite difficult to obtain as the mere filing of a notification to apply constitutes itself an infraction of the Motor Vehicle Code, albeit minor.

Fern, Fern; how could I tell her what lay ahead? And the recently rein-
stated sodomy laws of Sawyer Hogg (a source of great civic pride and
ingenuous fellow feeling among us) were among the most strict of all
the Small Worlds. Fern, gender-bended.

Fern, who henceforth would not know whether to sit fetchingly
with legs crossed, or in manly fashion, spread wide with feet planted
squarely upon the solid earth. We decided to take a long walk into the
desert to think things through; we decided to do this even though polls
suggested the desert was a creepy, inhospitable place where the long
arm of democracy could not quite reach. There was something just a
little suspicious about the desert in our countrymen's eyes, and the
Parliament had even revoked the name of the place Cahoon's Quiet,
because of certain fears and suspicions concerning the maleficent implications of the desert, its nearly infinite prospects, solemn and hieratic
hoodoos perched on white linen limestone in the aquamarine blush of
sunset, its wild rivers of silvery clatter that roared for an hour then
dreamed for a decade; something there was here that evaded what I do
best, namely, count. Likewise, something in that vast, unseizable
emptiness could only chill the souls of our wily elders, those who had
framed the Originary Document in stalwart hickory, and tamed both
sawgrass and swamp, rolling prairie of purplish origami and gloomy
forest pilth, but who had seen deeply into the precincts of the enlightened human soul (from the time of Chaz the Destroyer) and like Sir
Isaac Newton with his gleaming calipers had measured and traced the
shape of all that lay there, mental landscape of prehistory, naked and
useless, paltry and barely educable. Was this doom our first disobedi-
ence, or merely a type of some primordial dereliction we could not
fathom and knew not the name of? Who could say? As the date
we dreaded approached we took our sacramental vows, adopted
a surname—against one of the most powerful taboos of Sawyer
Hogg—namely, "Cahoon", and commenced our long march
into the desert, regardless of what fate or bad weather might
spring on us.

🦇 🦇 *{Cahoon's Quiet—A Brief Digression}:*

Although Cahoon's Quiet occupies fully two-thirds of the known surface of Sawyer Hogg, she is largely an unknown terrain, for reasons hinted at above. The "Cahoon" of Cahoon's Quiet is thought to be one Mulciber P. Cahoon, inventor of the Pedalkick Floating Bootstrap and one of the richest men in the time before Eulalia, and before the revolt of the Colonial Guard that first set in motion our famous revolution. Cahoon, or the Mahoon of Cahoon, as he was affectionately known, was rumored to have bought votes in outlying regions of the Quiet, and in other cases simply stuffed ballot boxes with fictitious names and those of the dead, all with addresses deep in the inner regions of that mysterious wasteland, a place regarded then as now to be ill-omened, dangerous and haunted by ferocious werewolves, Limavady toads and tusked wererabbits. Cahoon understood no man could prove him wrong since no Sawyer Hodgian dared make the trek across that velvety stillness, where glistening licorice-hued vermiculite hissingly flows in strange river-like dunes beneath a ghostly violet sky. With forty percent of these empty seats, or "quiet seats", at his command, the Mahoon of Cahoon seemed poised, like the National Socialists of another far away Small World, to take control of the apparatus of governance for his own obscure purposes. His crime was only revealed, at the eleventh hour, when a visionary autodidact of the autochthonous VellyBelly people emerged from the edge of the Quiet, and once quietened with soporifics extruded from the lemony salve of the local caloroso shrub (a notorious truth serum) proclaimed the Quiet was indeed a total complete Quiet, and that the only human creature to be found in the whole variorum flatlandia of the Quiet (aside from Gertrude, his half-wit sister and amanuensis) was Song Man, whom he worried with worship over all the occult purlieus of the Quiet, and about whom nothing else was known. Except Song Man's status as demi-divinity; except for his strange Elmervian tendency to hats and the habit of biting; except for the collection of opaque aphorisms (Song Man's Solomonical Sequence) attributed to him, and a single

🦇 91

odd roundelay from the marches of the Sour East Quiet, most remote of all the border regions:

> Sharp knife cut most clean,
> Dull knife cut most deep;
> Sharp knife got no bean,
> Dull knife got no bone;
>
> Break my teeth, break my teeth
> on the old tombstone.

There it was we hid out in some stupendous caverns venturing forth during the night time only for water from a tiny spring located at the base of a strange hump of a nameless massif we dubbed "Fern's Fall". We managed to collect edible fungi from corners of the cave; and following their droppings, were able also to capture and slaughter wholesale a great variety of desert rodents, including Mocgan's rat, the three-toed green-tufted karst weasel, the Coleraine shabeen (a kind of short-haired tawny badger), and the exquisitely marked Sawyer Hodgian wolverine, which as elsewhere on our world is prepared with turnips and hot chilies in a stew, the aroma of which was said to have compelled the Great Originator to leave his deathbed for the last time—pity, the source of this aroma could not be located and our hero himself collapsed in a confusion of flailing and clattering, and died there quickly of multiple fractures after tumbling down all three flights of his summer house on Cape Fear, just off the pier in the roaring September surf of Lake Negotiation. This was hushed up in the first decades of the Second Republic, but as we are a keen-witted people when it comes to matters of shame and public humiliation, it could of course not be hushed up forever.

92

Thus our frugal repasts in our nameless cavern took on a peculiar patriotic coloring, particularly as the glassy, mica-flecked walls above our crude stone hearth reflected shapes from the daynight world without even as these merged with images of flames and our two, glaring, sooty faces framed in the half-light so fetchingly we resembled two refugees from a medievalist vision of Tophet. Still, our doom was inescapable it seemed; the date was set, and the line-item veto had been declared unconstitutional so even if the Chief Executive had been aware of our plight it was far from clear he would have responded (was this all, I wondered darkly, in the darkest of my dark hours, ranging around in the black oblivion of the cave's deepest, most forbidding regions, some kind of grotesque retribution for his refusal to take action, right after his first inaugural, on the vexing issue of gays in the military? No, I cried, hopelessly at odds, I do not want to go there). After some time I reconciled myself to the fact: Fern would indeed be refoliated, and among her divergences would be untoward androgyny. Androgyny, my foe.

Sure enough, the anomaly we had so long anticipated arrived. One day, as I arrived at the mouth of the cave my arms loaded with discarded wooden side-tables from the traditional student desk of Prehistory and Pre-prehistory, which we employed in our amateur theatricals, I sensed a new vibration. Something I had not perceived before, a sensation almost beyond the sense of perfect sense minims. Focussing all my attentions I thought I heard voices from within our now quite familiar sanctuary. Out of the corner of my eye, my fear-widened eye, I noticed something out of place in the total, planar visual field. Stepping forward, I heard wood and tin clatter. There at my feet, just to one side of my worn clogs lay a brightly gleaming beer can; and from within, the unmistakable sound of a college football game chattering on our portable shortwave.

🔅 🔅 🔅 *{Portosmithereens}:*

On the far side of Cahoon's Quiet, indeed on the opposing hemisphere of the Democratic Republic of Sawyer Hogg, clothed in mystery and cross-dressed in the scintillant costumery of late antiquity, lies nestled the metropolis of Portosmithereens, a place not on any map. The place is a rare instance of no place, because the people who live there reject all authority, as constituted by the protocols, affidavits and documentaria the Great Originator promulgated at Drumcreep, in Year One, hour of the parable of the Leopard of Prague. Now when Fern and I were boys, splashing about in creeks and ditches off the Interstate near Great Stephen and Little Stephen Park, we had never noticed that on maps that part of the world appeared null and void, cordoned off by a dotted line within which in the most innocuous of lettering one could notice the innocent though, in retrospect, odd legend: "Section 43/P short glass tail. No Assump." But it was here we emerged, my boy-bride and me after such a long haul from our Platonic cavern that even I was unable to count the days. No one here troubled us and we soon found work as brokers as the local commodities exchange market. Portosmithereens it turned out (like most of Medieval Europe) possessed no zero, and hence certain calculations proved difficult, and the outcome of others completely undecidable. This is where I came in, with my speedy and hence eponymous ability to count and tabulate; Fern, on the other hand, was a whiz at arranging, categorizing, and general office management. The Portosmithereensians were astonished by these skills, and soon we were the talk of the town. Before we arrived all transactions, of every conceivable kind, involved direct exchange and barter, often with consequences that seemed to us, cradled in democracy as we were and thus numerically enlightened, to be the nadir of barbarism. Can you imagine, for example, a man pushing his front porch down Main Street in order to exchange it for a sack of potatoes?

94

Likewise, before we arrived, it must be admitted the fashion quotient of Portosmithereens approached and frequently exceeded the grotesque. Lacking any clear sense of identity intelligence, or sense of barest numeracy the inhabitants had no problem with mismatched shoes and stockings; indeed, they had not the foggiest notion of why these and other items were issued in pairs, and not manufactured and sold singly. Color-coordination meant nothing to them so that stripes and spots in random arrangement seemed perfectly okay; not to mention garish combinations of black and blue, orange and avocado, licorice and banana. Often otherwise sophisticated Portosmithereensians would wear their Armani suits neatly pulled inside-out because that was how they found them in the morning. This sort of alternation of inside-out, outside-in provided a rudimentary system for telling days apart, a project whose intellectual underpinnings they seemed able to grasp only in fits and starts. We never did figure out their sexual habits which may not be so surprising since they apparently possessed none. Of course sex they had and clearly suffered no diminution (their young were everywhere in evidence, mewling, howling and banging on tin cans with wooden soup spoons); but they seemed literally not to have formed any hard and fast concepts regarding the whys and wherefores of the whole thing. Mostly they were kind, warm and generous. I don't remember any of their names (except for one) because they kept changing them, and moved frequently from house to house. Mostly they were blond with eerie blush-bluish eyes, and about my height in spans (Fern being slightly shorter). But there is a story I must retell about one among them, the one whose name I did manage to remember, because it was an odd and creepy name, Gemma.

Gemma was a pretty young woman, as Fern used to be, and like Fern her long red hair tumbled down her back like a cartoon of DaVinci (who is DaVinci?); but Gemma one day discovered—in the usual way, by gazing into the deep and empty image of herself as she accidentally stumbled upon Lake Lady Slipper, a particularly mysterious and witchified place cupped neatly in the lesser of the two peanut shaped craters high atop Mount Ballyshoo in the neighboring state of New Botheration—primal

95

discord. As she gathered her own golden light into her inmost self, her convexity of consciousness, she delighted and delighted also in her delight as young persons have always done (certainly this was the case with Fern and me in our innocence) if they are good looking, not afflicted by chronic poverty or vile afflictions such as Foot Drop or Crandell's dementia (itself a variety of Radebaugh's Ruination). As she arose, however, Gemma found herself vexed by a doubt. That doubt took on form and shape. That doubt developed into a full-blown thought, and this thought diverged from all the rest of Gemma's more or less liberal, more or less democratically arrived at, mentation. Simply put, Gemma differed with herself. That divergence of self from self could not be easily negotiated because there was no one available to arbitrate Gemma's difference with herself. She fluttered and dove headlong into the lake of her despair, an inner lacuna and not an outer phenomenon, and thus not one easily negotiable, like the silvery waters of Lake Lady Slipper.

Gemma, always a pretty and a happy child, had been the delight of her friends and family, and an eyeful of their invested apple. Her difference from herself divided her also from others. What she gave with one hand, she withdrew with the other; what she celebrated from one side of her mouth, she castigated from the other; whom she loved one moment, she hated the next; what gods she worshipped at dawn, the denied at dusk; what fashion caused her to coo one day, she reviled and deplored the day after; what political cause she championed sooner, she did her utmost to subvert and destroy later as time rolled around, like a ball, and lay there upon her pale, open palm. For the truth was Gemma was so evenly at odds with herself, Gemma contra Gemma, that nothing could break the tie vote. Gemma was, as it were, hemispherically divided and in this aspect, now haggard, now blissful, caused all her friends, and those who loved her, one by one, to depart and leave her in deadlock, empty and alone in her interior lack of majority rule. All but one, because in my youth I did accomplish one good thing, Gemma's trust. Because to me her very lack of certainty, her refusal to accept the popular cant and opinion of the moment, gave her a freshness that I missed in all others.

She would make up words.

She would laugh at her own folly, and that of others without claiming to know the answers to the questions she posed; nor would she disguise her fanatic opinions as questions to conceal an unpalatable agenda, in a data-burst of feigned humility.

In her dreams, night after night, she wandered in the floral amazement of the mythical gardens of Eulalia, and would catch a sparrow in her fist and let it go unharmed. She knew that if a lion could speak we would not understand what it said.

And she trusted me, for I was slow and ugly in those days, even though called Quickness.

Gemma's beauty was disturbing to most because you could not put your finger on it. Her beauty was a vibratory continuum, something about the center of it deliciously unstill. She and my dear Fern resembled each other in the wild redness of their hair, the ripple of their bodies, walking, running, climbing in trees after being forbidden to. I could never recapture, in either girl, the exact color of the eye, the hue of golden, freckle-speckle arm and back. And when Gemma went away I was very sad. I should not have been, for as I later learned she had not truly vanished or expired, but only suffered a rare and wonderful metamorphosis.

So: now Gemma is changed, changed at a Seven-Eleven, late one night in August, on the shores of Lake Lady Slipper; changed by an unknown god, according to Cantor's Rule, into an unusual species of peach, the Peekaboo Semilion Pluperfect Peach (because she had been a peach of perfection if ever there was).

No one consulted me on the matter.

And the lemma of Gemma's dilemma follows me, tumbling down the tangle of all the red-haired days that follow, one upon the other. Days that I have taken it upon myself to count, if only to keep an open space within, as I rush, rush and rush; as the world whistles by.

◗ ◗ ◗ ◗ *{Festina Lente—Hurry Up Slowly}:*

The upshot of my friendship with Gemma was that I slowed, grew roundy and circumspect, almost a stone. Another lemma of Gemma's dilemma was that I was bound thereby (was there a subcommittee somewhere, deep within the Sawyer Hodgian boxwood, devoted to such matters?) to fall in love with Fern when the time rolled around at last, like another ball. In any case Fern foliated and divulged androgyny and we made an escape to the tents and minarets of Portosmithereens, a place where unfashionable differences could be delved, even and especially if their hemispheres, whether of precious dewy peach or of some other family of apple, or an eyeful of some other other, were helplessly divided against, within or together amongst themselves. Delight's differences with herself summon up antitypes and other tiptoes that barely tap on the floors of Fern's dimmed hallways as they glide, glide in a silence no sanctimonious council of elders could possibly stifle or control.

We would have stayed there together perhaps forever, bigwigs in Portosmithereens, but one day a messenger arrived on the post road, and stepped out of his battered 1937 LaSalle, covered with the glittering dust of Cahoon's Quiet; I stepped forward, fearing the worst; my hands shook so badly I could not open the telegram, but only clawed at it ineffectually. But the messenger himself assisted, and Fern read the contents first silently, then aloud. No one among that crowd understood; no one understood what a Supreme Court was, much less a Supreme Court decision. But Fern and I understood only too well.

Fern, alas, was to be changed back; she made a better girl than a boy, the Supreme Court had decided, and we were

98

requested to return to our ancestral homestead on the slopes of Mount General Rumor, and there to take up the burden of our domestic bliss.

No one consulted me.

So we returned home, and to the Klein Bottle of our former love, even if no one asked me.

bup

bup

HORROCKS
(and TOUTATIS too)

Because I was a very tall young girl, every time I would walk along the Charcoal Road a group of short and brutish boys would pelt me with stones. I say "because" but I really do not know. I had done nothing wrong to them and very tall girls certainly have the same rights as short and brutish boys, among these the right to walk unhindered down the old Charcoal Road.

Was it because in a former life I had fallen in love with a toucan from Toutatis? I am talking about the time when our world, Horrocks and his world, Toutatis, were one, each nestled cozily in the embrace of the other. Before Eulalia, I would say, and her disturbing revelations about our common origins, and before the snickersnee of doubt had undone the primal innocence of our world. Because of our unique rupture and separation from Toutatis and her lovely toucans, Eulalia imagined her message with its fervor and ferretry, its apocalyptic dislexsia and cosmic dyspepsia, would be an easier sell here on Horrocks than on Elmer, Muazzez or 1965 UU. But the One Worldy hypothesis is an idea out of tune with time, has lost a center, one might say, or any fundamental gravitation allure. The old centripetal shell-game. We, the dwellers of the Small Worlds have for some time been serious and dedicated centrifugalists, and any opposing scripture or line of argument we approach with an intrinsic and innate skepticism, as though it were only the latest news from the bughouse. Many of us, in fact, are rabidly pugilistic centrifugalists and more harm would be done to and among ourselves were it not the case that when excited or enraged we tend to fly rapidly apart, centrifugally, one from the other no matter which small world we hail from, whether it be Wu, Flea, or Linda Susan. You can call me Pollen. Pollen is what was named by my parents in the olden times before Toutatis broke off from Horrocks, and went wilding off the plane of the ecliptic, hideho!, like a wild child on a bicycle with two square wheels, a candidate for the Half-Wit's Hall of Fame.

Pollen, you will say, why Pollen?

Because, I suppose, my parents had their hopes that even though I was in love with a toucan from Toutatis, given the fact that I was a very tall dandelion of a girl, I might one day pollinate correctly; that I might one day flower and spread. Flower and spread as they had never done. For quite early on in my life I learned that I was not their natural child, but had been rescued from a public trash receptacle near the town of Stopped Cold, a seaside resort situated on the Horse Latitudes of Horrocks and a place well-know for its high fashion low-life.

Origins again, damnable origins.

Because I would just as soon be done with all this bother of origins as pollinate, and if it were up to me I would be done with all names also, even my own. Names hem in a person and constitute a kind of rebuke. A name speaks the person who is named thereby, and constitutes a boundary. I would prefer not to be known by a name even one of my own devising, especially one of my parents' devising.

bup

Back, way back when, when my fly-book was a brittle-star of fluorite, things I imagine were different. Borders and boundaries were simple taunts or tautologies. To be was a dance of flutes and flutter-lines and the continual breakdown of three coplanar curves by nomographics. Out of respect for my parents I referred to them simply as X and Y, interchangeably. Because to my mind they were interchangeable.

As the story goes my parents, X and Y, went fishing one time out near the Strewn Area on the Nombril River at a point roughly equidistant between Fess Point and Base Point. This was in the middle of winter, and winter on Horrocks wins the Nobel Prize in the category of general down and out no good. You freeze your tits off, grow icicles on the tip of your nose and cannot see worth a nock noggin because of all the oily precipitates hanging low, just above the spidery-bramble and soapstones. They intended to drill down through the ice with an A-type triple-bit overshot steam drill:

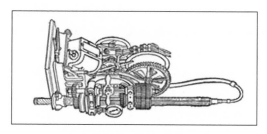

X and Y were experts at night-fishing for Horrockian noodlefish, a rare delicacy in and around the Horse Latitudes, and even beyond. Noodlefish are as slippery as a Nootka sprocket, and you have to have high marks in ice-fishing even to get near one. But on this occasion the noodlefish nobbled both X and Y—I cannot recall whether or not I was around at all or had not yet been adopted (and the main course of nobble had not even been served).

What X and Y mistook for the frozen middle of the mighty Nombril river was in fact not a river at all. They were not anywhere near that place because they incorrectly deciphered the maps, and were miles off in the middle of the Nombril's adjacent floodplain, a place known as Perfecto Non Troppo and rumored to be the quietest pace in the world. But this they did not know, as they set briskly about erecting their fabulous machinery. Soon however as the triple-bit steam drill began to chew up and spit out long and gluey worms of organic and inorganic material they began to suspect a problem: Where was the Nombril River? Where had she gone? Consult the cartography. The cartography indicates our present location to be correct ergo.

Someone must have buried the lake as though it were a dead dog. Now why should someone take the trouble to bury a large, fluvial body of water as though it had no business being where it was and constituted only an obnoxious eyesore? The truth is that Horrockians of every stripe have a mania for burying what you will according to the flutter-kick of whim as occasion, that fickle whore, permits and especially when no-one is looking. But while we are maniacs at burying and artful forgetfulness we are not nearly so keen on digging up, and other fine arts of retrieval. Our dislike of borders and boundaries such as the oppressive terminus of the grave and all things gravely compels us in contradictory compulsion, for our need, like the fashion in hemlines, must go only so low, only so low and no further.

bupbup

But let me take a moment to digress on the One-Worldy Hypothesis, and why we of Horrocks including me, one Pollen, find the possibility so jarring even despite the Revelation of Eulalia. Because one thing you discover if you are a very tall young girl in a world of short and brutish boys is that even and especially if you do not believe in differences, differences like that between X and Y, ends and beginnings, real and imaginary numbers, the right and the left hand, the fact that someone else does has a way of forcing the issue. You have no choice but to share the world of difference foisted upon you as though it were a fact accomplished.

The One Worldy people are always talking about how, in the old days, people could travel far and wide and enjoy the pleasure of socializing in places; outlandish places where people not only behaved strangely, but were strange—deeply, helplessly, irredeemably strange. You could not begin to figure them out because you could not understand what they were saying and doing. You could not figure out what they were trying to accomplish by all their strange behavior because to you it looked like they didn't know what they were doing or had gotten it all wrong or were putting you on or were just doing whatever random stuff as came into their fuzzy head to see what you would do (and so on, infinite regress); and drive you crazy. Naturally if you were one of us, normal, and not a One Worldy type, you would return the favor, and so on, infinite regress. But, maintain the One Worldy folk, despite all this you can break through and establish a connection if and only if you treated people not as one of you (or one of us, one might say), but make no assumptions at all so that the lack of common ground might itself be a basis for further, and more fruitful intercourse.

We of Horrocks could never buy that.

Because. Because. Because.

I suppose we could not buy that because the thing about boundaries is that once you have one you must perforce deal with what or whomever is to be found on the other side. Why is that? Because a boundary functions like a line drawn in the sand, or in the snow of our midwinter Horrockian hush; to yield to such definition seems an affront, however nebulous and random, to identity itself.

Pollen, you say.

Pollen, I say. But alas I am becoming lost like a lion rampant in the golden spray of my own random variation, in my own very tall girl display.

So: Back to X and Y and their apparatus likewise lost on the vast midwinter flood plain of the Nombril, namely Perfecto Non Troppo, the quietest place ever known. As they drilled and drilled and still detected no ice and certainly no ice water, their anxiety began furiously to rub forelegs together, like a fly in the face of the fly agaric. Unaware of their inability to read simple pictorial representations of the earth and heavens, and unsure of what to do, X and Y joined in an equation of horror, for they had encountered a border. That of human ignorance and misapplied know-how. Attaching a lazy-tong to the bit assembly they decided to drill deeper, deeper, deeper down into the Horrockian crust. Very quickly it because apparent to them that somehow the river had eluded them, but what they did discover in its place drew them on, curiouser and curiouser.

Layer upon layer of strange stuff was revealed. First, just beneath the half frozen loam and semi permea-dermeable mat of grass and twigs and crushed dead mice, they encountered a strange layer that when carefully examined turned out to consist entirely of crushed lightbulbs; then another, equally distinct, of crushed Campbell soup cans. Then another of good luck charms, talismans and so on. Then a layer of hats, berets and tam-o'-shanters; one of old toothbrushes, one of whistles and flutophones; one of wandering Jew in warming pans; one of starling feathers and dried starfish. Then screws and screwdrivers; the next, rings of all kinds including both wedding and boxing. Illuminated manuscripts which gave off a soft, lilac glow that changed the hue of all that came near; old dry cells and batteries; a very thick layer of law books and legal documentaria of every conceivable variety, and on and on.

What silence of silence, what drowsy form of mass amnesia had they discovered? My parents decided to consult with those more knowing, professors at the local beanery, Dromedary University. Owing to fickle fashion, on Horrocks strict analysis and vertical exegesis had been about as much a growth industry as soft boiling Dresden eggs. X and Y's discovery changed all that. Hoping to realize a quick profit from their accidental misreading, my parents turned over their claim to a crowd of experts. Before long they were toasted and feted up and down the length of the Nombril River, a place they had been unable to locate. My selfish parents used their trunkloads of "choke cherry blots" (as the Horrockian legal tender, the *Horoi*, was commonly called, because of its comparative worthlessness) to buy an excursion aboard to the steamship "Kowloon" not only throughout all the tributaries of the Nombril, but further South into regions of gloomy tropical splendor, where few Horrockians had ever ventured. The "Kowloon" was decorated with paper lanterns, and a jazz band played late into the night as that insubstantial pleasure craft (the "Kowloon", like many vessels dating from before the catastrophic break-away of Toutatis, was made almost entirely of silkweed, cardboard and woven horse-tail fronds) drifted on, and on and on; so that even as they sipped martinis and danced the Chandler Wobble their name became synonymous with self indulgence, and a devotion to the things of this poor excuse of a world that would have shamed the moralists of old, whether One-Worldy and visionary or Orthodox and devoted to the adoptive pleasures of privation and dismantling of all things public.

On and on the "Kowloon" drifted, a shadowy blotch of hedonism lost in the murk of a South leprous with unpurged need and desire. By accident, and is it any wonder? the Orthodox among us would add, they passed insensibly over the impermeable dotted line that separates Moth County from the rest of Horrocks, only to emerge eleven days later—penniless and mere-shadows of their former selves, in broken sandals, their hideho glad rags and smoking jackets caked with swamp muck, and torn to shreds—on the soft shoulder of the dog end, you guessed it, of the old Charcoal Road about a mile and half from the Rite Aid at Stopped Cold where you know who had been dropped just hours before, screaming bloody murder and wrapped in the business section of the Tarpon Springs *Tourniquet*, a periodical I make a point of never reading. Ah, but the forbidden *mbisimo* of Moth County and poison powder of her silent wings cannot so easily be washed away.

bupbup bup

Imagine me with Cerenkov effect coming up and off me like steam off a water barrel deep in the black lagoon. Ah, but what happened then and there is far less important to this polygon ramble than the silks of pollination earlier, much earlier in the days before I was devised, under what aegis, before the break-away and departure of Toutatis and my beloved aboard her as we both watched, both tyros of separation and attachment. Birds of the feathery after-pull of the heart half-spoken. For, in those days, I was a little touraco of the family *Musophagidae*, and my postmodern plumage entranced all who saw. My wing bit the wind as I danced both high and low. We flew over and above all of the little world of Horrocks, and knew the place better than any person ever would. Our pleasure in each other's company was intense and recipro-cal, being birds of a feather, even on those certain occasions when there came a strangeness between us that bordered on a chill. The chill of recognition of the self. The chill of recognition of the self in the stranger, and the stranger in the self. George, I would say, because that was the name of my beloved, George, why do you pout and clack your bill so flatly, flatly and with hollow dullness as if it were a broken transom blown back and forth by an ill wind against its frame? But George would not reply, only his bill would glow softly and to my eyes at least, seem to enlarge as if through a sudden infusion of deep emotion. A surpassing of emotional surplus. Then we would leap from the twisted limb of our favorite haunt, an ancient Susanna bush, one whose growth had been all her life at best a last-ditch struggle again the fierce otherworldly winds of Jeptha's Pipe, a mouth-shaped cavernous declivity to the north of the Strewn Area, and famous in the early days of Horrocks as the voices of all the ages past, present and future, commingled in such a way that only adepts of the Poison Oracle (*Mbisimo*) could make sense of that tantalizing, lily-tongued polyphony. We would leap and fly as gracefully as possible—easier said than done when you are a toucan whose fabulous bill, though cosmetically all triumph, must almost over-match poor George's stumpy wings. O, his dear little double somethings that seemed to resemble wings in appearances rather than actually be them; double somethings like the fenders of an automobile or the unseen backstage area on either side of the stage of a proscenium theater, or the enlarged pectoral fins of the flying fish (flying fish, asks Pollen, what in the name of wintergreen is that?), or a double airfoil arrangement each of which is symmetrically positioned to the side of an airplane fuselage.

Darting over the flat side of Horrocks, all pyrite and lead flow as that dips over at an angle so extreme as to nearly sicken any merely human sensibility. We flew in cautionary tandem. Because it must be admitted that there is something within the human inner ear that becomes woozy at the slightest sudden swoop whether of gyrocopter or gypsy moth.

Darting over the flat side of Horrocks, and then to topple nearly three hundred degrees, over and over and overfold, to the pleasant valleys and pasture lands of Lime Twig, Top o' the Line, String Bean and other notable places of Horrocks in our time of innocence before the arrival of Eulalia and her infernal croaking rabble—this constituted for us avians quite a thrill. We would nestle against each other, rub each other's bill and do the best we could to smarten up the other's plumage. Horrocks seemed a happy place because it never occurred to us that half the damn thing might just break off, like a dead branch in a thunderstorm and plop down and rush away into a figurative Nombril River which is a mad torrent, full of stumps, sawhorses, saddlebags, snowshoes, basketballs and hollow gourds from the Telegu people who used to raise their tents across the marches of Teasel, a place we avoided as there was nothing good to eat there, either for Touraco or Toucan.

As for the mistake itself, it was an accident and neither George nor I dreamed the consequences might turn out so alarming. George, you see, was fond of acorns and his very favorite ones grew atop an old, centuries old cypress perched on a notch at the very brink of Jephtha's Pipe. I confess I always thought this was a particularly spooky place and if it were up to me, we never would have come near, but then I was doing my best to make my truelove happy. Anyhow, George had this very large acorn in his bill, but for all his exertions the thick-walled thing simply wouldn't crack, for the life of me I don't get the taste for dried nuts. He became frustrated and carried the recalcitrant nut way, way, way up in the sky with the intention of flinging it down, hard, against one of the crags on the tippy, tippy top of Jephtha's Pipe; but once aloft he began to circle about curiously, as if the thin air of that great height had somehow affected his judgement. Soon he was so high up I could barely make out his shape, and I got worried. He might pass out and fall to his death, unconscious. Then too the diabolical howling of the wind might have done something to his sense of direction; it was certainly making me feel batty. So I yelled, yelled as loud as I could, "George, George, what are you doing up there?" And I could see that he heard me, because he took a sharp jerk to the left, as if to hear better; so I repeated myself, this time as loud as an out-of-breath touraco can manage which is pretty loud; and that pretty loud became louder still because somehow where I was hovering seemed to be exactly the right place as my shriek echoed and re-echoed strangely off the stony rampart of the Pipe. Now I could see him jolt, as if surprised by the astonishing amplitude of my voice, and as he jerked about he dropped the fatal acorn.

I watched it fall with him hard after; trying, zigzagging in the mad attempt, to intercept the damn thing; but no, the acorn dropped like a plumb-bob in an empty well. Oops, he said and that was the last thing I ever heard my beloved toucan say: Oops. Because the mighty acorn smacked the crags and somehow dislodged a boulder that, likewise, plummeted drastically down, taking half the apex of the Pipe with it, the whole mass, by this time a cubic mile or two, crunching and rolling down into the mouth of the declivity itself. This was followed, in a moment or two by such fiery shocks and detonations as I had never heard before. You've guessed by this time I imagine the rest of the story: how detonation after detonation cracked the peaceful little world and shattered our happy, seemingly stable carrot patch. In a few days the seismic activity had reached such a pitch that all of us on Horrocks, avians and humans alike, thought the classic horror movie tumult we found ourselves in the midst of was in truth the fat lady's song. As the world of Toutatis bid ours farewell in a display of pyrotechnics for all the ages, I recall in an upper corner of that apocalyptic canvas, a trio of very small, sad toucans waving their red handkerchiefs on sticks; waving forlornly as the world beneath their bony little three-toed feet began to break away.

Ah, Pollen how your ambiguous and morally neutral dust supplies anthers to the stigma of questions no god-fearing Horrockian had the wit to pose unless under prompt by one of Eulalia's screeching crows. But who are they, those crows, to polka dot? When all of them, a random sample of my fellows Horrockians, I mean, were chasing after the Eulalian rapture and kissing the hem of her skirt, I shied away, feigned girlish modesty, and considered deeply on the One-Worldy theory:

CONSIDER: Could there have existed one world large enough to contain all the myriad hodge-podge of small worlds, innumerable in the opinion of the learned? Perhaps, but not likely.

CONSIDER: Could such a hypothetical single world manage to contain such a bulk of iron and stone, such an awful magnitude of mass that the wild centripetal forces within would not crush the magnifico like a maharanee style dish causing the whole shabeen (shall we name the awful hypothetical, "Eulalia", after her who first pronounced the theme, and spread the word from small world to small world undiminished?); causing the whole of Eulalia to collapse in upon herself, and drop out of the sky as a plumb-bob in an empty well drops, forever, who knows where? Indeed, would not such a world being a very large world, a large and very tall one, be intrinsically short-lived, a monster of nature? Drastically unstable?

CONSIDER: As a corollary of this: Could such a place possibly exist, or have ever existed, where people of all different shapes and sizes and similitudes gather at once and to all appearances not only get along, but actually flourish? I doubt it. I more than doubt it; I deny it because my experience on Horrocks is such that difference seems universally to constitute a threat, however you pretty it up with talk of fellowship and the family of man and cantrips of the One-Worldy among us, all fifth columnists of a universalist hegemony with an alien and therefore unknowable agenda.

That is why I, one long tall girl with the curious name of Pollen, do not buy this apocalyptic anamnesis. When I do the Chandler Wobble, I dance with my own shadow and like it that way; when I bathe in the soft glow of the Cerenkov effect, it is my own Cerenkov effect I bathe in, and not some wig-trip of a loose screw from the People's Republic of Jesus Shell Bean, nor the Sheriff of Choisy-le-Roi, nor the fall guy of Tansy's Tanagram, nor Tapir of Gordon the Angel, nor the fairy ring of Studebaker Lodgepole Mohacs, nor the round dance of Arsine the African Violet.

Sameness is the matchless excess of my own similitude, and the only boundary I bow to is my own native glow, both decorative and decretive. All talk of the other reminds me of the horrors of Moth County and the stubborn futility of my parents, X and Y, whom we left, feet frozen in the midwinter hush of the quietest place ever known some distance from the Nombril River, whose intertwined windings and interlaced meanderings are said to form a script that can be read from as far as Sawyer Hogg at the Sub-Horrocks Point when that other, odd small world pays a brief visit to these precincts every eleven thousand four hundred and sixty two years; for X and Y entrenched in their folly had reached a point of lunatic intorsion so mimetic that upon penetration of the fifty-third layer (that of pencil leads and Lincoln pennies) they noticed a curious phenomenon they failed to report to the equally lunatic professors of Dromedary University, what at first seemed only an accidental and meaningless repetition, but proved to be far, far more than that. The 54th layer consisted, you see, of broken lightbulbs, and the 55th followed with a suspiciously familiar one of crushed Campbell soup cans, and so on; the sedimented remains of prehistoric Horrocks appeared, after a certain fateful and sulphurous point, TO REPEAT BOTH IN ORDER AND KIND.

Mineral history on an infinite loop; nay, as an infinite loop.

An infinite loop of facts and seasons, of annular rings of growth and sun-spatter, of dumbfoolery and Torwell-colored decay. So, as I reckon it, my parents must have been half-maddened by this murderous new knowledge which may explain some of the odd doings, in between the inevitable martinis aboard the rickety "Kowloon" as she crept through the early morning murk, approaching near, far too near, the allegorical and pharoanic mists of Moth County. Perhaps Zeus Herkimer, the obscene and paro-dist divinity whose crimes and misdemeanors so often resulted in the primitive system of borders and boundaries (also horoi) that so tormented and plagues our ancestors, had played one more caustic and senseless trick, a trick for which both my parents and I, not to mention all my confreres on Horrocks, would inevitably pay; but pay in what coin, whether in classical "horoi"—choke cherry blots—, or in some stranger, newer coin?

bupbup bupbup

Just as senseless repetition seems to be the lot of Horrockian geol-ogy, an equally senseless lack of consistency seems to be mine. Every road I take seems blocked by Zeus Herkimer and the glittery stones he leaves to warn those who approach. The way is blocked and impassible, an absolute inenerrable dead end. So that the only story left to me is the one I am trapped in and cannot escape, the story of Zed, the conclud-ing variable in my tragic algebra.

Deafened by my hatred of Eulalia and all things universalist and One-Worldy, I took up with skin-heads from the Strewn Area, which was the name applied to the placed formerly the footprint of the renegade world of Toutatis. A few shabby settlements had sprung up there, mostly trailer parks and shantytowns, roughneck howl huddles with names like Shaggy and Violation and Duh. And I would travel in an old wreck of a silver airstream with hooligans from Huh, the scariest of these. We would put on little anti One-Worldy shows, with live music and a frankly pretty depressing side-shows with voice-over and hand puppets, which was where I came in since I had some familiarity with these from my family, or Y's side of the family as they were a loud and pretentious bunch of ex-showbiz people, used to the catbird seat so to speak and it, I guess, rubbed off on me. One of them, Y_3, an uncle or something, had a way with hand puppets.

Deep in the forests of Moth County, forests so strange and still no image can collect the mysterious glow of what grows there, lies the even stranger town of Silvery with her famous Puppet Theater. All Horrockians love puppets and puppet theaters, but most of these are crude and vulgar, and the shows they enact similarly crude and vulgar, mostly consisting of adaptations of our lesser classics. These stories are mostly bloody and grotesque version of stories from more sophisticated places, where storytellers had managed to lend some dignity to the narratives they constructed and not just smash them together indifferently. Boiled Tom was always a favorite, and the Tale of the Walking Cranberry Bog. But the Puppet Theater of Silvery was indeed a silvery and silken thing. The stories were all whispered in your ear so softly and gracefully, as if by a cat, you barely knew they were happening; the puppets' odd way of expression so delicate and odd, both inexplicably vague and deeply moving, that no one could ever really describe them to someone who had not been present (at least until now). Indeed, among theater-goers there were sometimes arguments between parties of those who had witnessed the same show, but were unable to come to any conclusion concerning the nature of what they had just seen. It was as if there was something about the nature of the shows presented there that elicited deep and inexpressible thoughts and feelings from each and every theater-goer, thoughts and feelings that were so deep and strange that they resisted easy formulation into the quotidian language of cause and effect. Nor could any of the theater-goers even agree on such incidental details as the title of the piece they had just attended, nor on the number of players in the cast, nor what color were the sets and lights, nor what the costumes looked like, nor on the length of the performance and whether the story ended well or badly for their hero and heroine.

All people could agree on was the sensation of silk moving

slowly and languidly. Moving this way and that, in drapery, in curtains with tassels and lacy filigree of hues so complex and iridescent they seemed to give off illumination without the instrumentality of normal theater lighting, a distinct impossibility of course. Of the marionettes themselves, opinion was similarly divided, though most audience members claimed to be deeply affected by the realism of the eyes, eyes which seemed to take in all of the world that lay about them but at the same time to see nothing. Marionettes at the same time possessed of the most intense, penetrating vision, and the holy blindness of the wisest of the Old Ones from before the time of Eulalia.

Y_3 himself was a self-proclaimed cynic and burnt-out case, a man who believed in nothing, for whom the mystic forests of deepest Moth County were only an endless aggregation of clothing racks and trees, all of which were decked out with an infinity of old suits and hats and overcoats, mostly in muted shades of velvety gray and pale rose-taupe, all of it quietly rotting away, a paradise only for the lovely insects for whom the county was named. Y_3 said there was only one story played in the Puppet Theater of Silvery, and what it boiled down to was this:

A man with no name or with one withheld could not be content within the confines of his own little room, with his cozy bed, fireplace and little brass rabbit on the window sill. One night he awoke from a dream, a dream the horror of which was that he could not awake from it, and in order to comfort himself began to throw more and more wood on the fire. The flames grew higher and the heat within his little iron furnace grew more and more intense. But the dancing flames had bewitched him, and he could not stop. Finally he threw into the inferno a green and greeny Horrockian cypress stump of the sort George and I had discovered clasping the crags at the very pinnacle of Jeptha's Pipe. Very quickly this too caught horribly on fire, and the oily air pockets trapped within began to howl like voices of the damned. Then the thing exploded with tremendous force, and all the little flamelets ran out of the iron contraption, out of the chinks in the wall and under the door and around the window frame. Now the man sits alone in the dark, as the room cools slowly about him. On the wall a cut silhouette of his lost love hangs, Eulalia. But in the dark no one can make out the features of her face. After a while the man without a name goes back to bed, climbs into it, and goes to sleep.

He dreams, all over again, of the silken marionettes of the Puppet Theater of Silvery in Moth County, which he had loved when he visited there as a boy. And of the time even before that, when he and a group of brutish boys took to pelting, pelting with stones, a strange and tall young girl that they saw walking down the Charcoal Road.

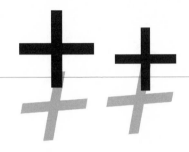

EPILOGUE:
LINDA SUSAN

fragments from: LINDA SUSAN: [5]

○○○ ○○○ ○○●
○○○ ○○○ ○○○
○○○ ○○○ ○○○   ...X{Y}.

○○○ ○○○ ○○●
○○○ ○○○ ○○●
○○○ ○○○ ○○○   ...phee—wild hair—

○○○ ○○○ ○○●
○○○ ○○○ ○○●
○○○ ○○○ ○○●   Displicip.

○○○ ○○○ ○○●
○○○ ○○○ ○○●
○○○ ○○○ ○●●   ...Azure, bluebird's egg, the blue of the sands of
LINDA SUSAN. Our Prophetess, Eulalia, visited
this place early in the Age of Charm, just after the
Age of Doubt and...

---

[5] LINDA SUSAN is a small, bright world. An P-type planetoid composed of
pulverized bluish talc. Number 2683. Magnitude 13.00. Discovered 26
November 1964. Named for L. S. Gray (aetat four, daughter of P.L. Gray who
first verified its existence. The following fragments were found, encoded
(in the cipher pProspero) on a piece of yellowing newsprint, *(Farrago
Freeman, vol. CXIII, no. 117, March 8, 1946)* and glued to the bottom of a
children's school desk found discarded by the side of the road, Route Nine,
just North of Saratoga, New York on 11 March, 1995. Edited by M.S.
Crowe, Cardinal of the College of Pataphysics at Molossus University, Dead
Snake Junction, Ohio.

And her dog, Wow.

They [Eulalia and Wow?] found these things to be self-evident: [..?..]...

...and clicked her silver heels three times in recognition of the truths uncovered in that place, the blue sands caressed by the silvery simoom of LINDA SUSAN.

LINDA SUSAN [Said Eulalia? Said Wow?] is *perfect* because of what she lacks: attorneys, real estate... [people?], purveyors of the dream... {[low?]... (i.e. the triple motto of Post-post, sad, sublunar Terra: Aim low, shit floats and the squeaking wheel gets the grease.)—Crowe .044}} and...

...and thereby avoids the tyranny of the ostensible. The tyranny of those who make lists who [...][cackle!?] begin every day by making a list of things to do, checking off each item as it is accomplished, those who [...][cackle!?] equate political freedom with the... making of lists.

ALL Linda Susans realize one must attack the problem of happiness, contextually, as a political imperative. As a series of nested political impera-tives... [One within the other? Onion? Egg? A system of scaleable social structures—scale within scale?—Crowe .047]

Accordingly, they do not NAME what is most high, or what is most low, else it... [wiggle?]. Else it be caused...[By us?—Crowe .049) to wiggle and mock its nature, and thus become something else.

They pray to no god, but... X{Y}...

...(that) a predicate is implied, an object of care or concern. Only that it be ethically undecidable what it is... (i.e.that *object*) in each specific instance— without reference to a *specific context*—in each specific context.

...they (The Linda Susans) care for detail, minutiae, the small things of the world of Linda Susan. Further than that they will not go.

...[Eulalia? Wow?]... understood the genius of their system as embodied in the... some laws are written and some are not; only the great FOOL imagines he/she/it [the low dream?] [...][cackle!?] can create anything solely by an ACT of writing.

Azure... in the interest of treating all other being [People? {The Fez?}—Crowe .077] as an absolute, a *Benevolent Foreigner*, an absolute of unknowable creation

[Entelechy?—Crowe .078]. An equal, regard-ing whom nothing is to be assumed, but warm, steamy breath and bright eyes...   ++ 121

...too many assumptions... X{Y}...
[Pineapples? Artichokes?—Crowe .079]

...for whom [The citizens of LINDA SUSAN?—
Crowe .099] *NOTHING* is to be assumed, as even
the weight [Feather-weight?—Crowe .101] of a
wrong name can crumple the brow of a god.

They honor women before and after childbearing
years (even) and great chefs.

(Their) political structures are temporary, tents rather
than mausoleums...

(Their) most primordial given [LINDA SUSAN
herself?—Crowe .477]—in the sense of a clearing in
the world, being alive—is of course not the world in
the sense of our determinate, substantive horizons;
instead it is an open region ["({O}Possum) Playing
Field" in the original Linda Susan—untranslatable in
the demotic patois of the

Americans—Crowe .478]: not of beings, but rather
of these horizons themselves.

...(They?) play tricks [Practical jokes?—Crowe .667]
on each other constantly, so that the trickery
[Wiggle?—Crowe .667] does not enter into the
realm of the most serious, the world of apparence,
the unnamed.

Eulalia came here, and was pleased and so did her dog, Wow. Wow was also pleased [Wag?—Crowe .669]

A single scorpion {[...][cackle!?]—Crowe .702} could destroy the entire world of LINDA SUSAN and often...

...could destroy LINDA SUSAN and often did. It was not a rich and famous place.

...It (LINDA SUSAN) was not a rich and famous place... since it *was*, however, fragile and its inhabitants would always be subject to the depredations of more powerful neighbors; but since they [The Linda Susans?—Crowe .713] bore no grudges [...][cackle!?] and valued... X{Y} [Horizon events?—Crowe .714]... more than the certainty of... plp-PoP-pu {[Verbal statuary?], [...][cackle!?]?—Crowe .715} they were always able to restore their ancient arts, disciplines, and other Joyous Practices {[... X(Y)...]?—Crowe .716} (Frequently they were ignored, and since they possessed nothing [Little of anything?—Crowe .717] anyone else... {[...][cackle!?]—Crowe .717} could understand the importance of [The *meaning* of?—Crowe .719] they were left pretty much alone.

One single demon... {[...][cackle!?]—Crowe .761} knows more than all of them, thought Eulalia, on her last visit here [There?—Crowe .768], during the Age of Hope. And so did her dog, Wow.

When I go [Eulalia? Wow?—Crowe .862] to Elmer I will not tell them about this place; nor when I go to Woo, 1965UU, Sawyer Hogg, Muazzez (The World of Hair), Mitake-Mura, Horrocks.

...nor on Ornamenta, Klotho or Wild; nor on any of the other Small Worlds, where My Words have, in general, fallen on on... the deaf [Unhearing? Unheeding?—Crowe .863]...

or on the ears of... the deaf [...][cackle!?]...

...or on Wow's [Bow-wow?—Crowe .977]...

...Azure sand... X{Y}...

The End

 *bup*

2000ANDWHAT?

An anthology of short stories about the turn of the millennium. What unifies these writers is their ability to avoid a predictable response to an inevitable event. Stories by Etel Adnan, Margaret Atwood, Frederick Barthelme, Lydia Davis, David Gilbert, Steve Katz, Kevin Killian, Donna Levreault, Harry Mathews, Ameena Meer, Susan Smith Nash, Niels Nielsen, Karl Roeseler, Teri Roney, Linda Rudolph, Kevin Sampsell, Lynne Tillman, Karen Tei Yamashita, Lewis Warsh, and Mac Wellman.
ISBN: 0-9639192-2-9 $12.00

FIVE HAPPINESS by David Gilbert

A short novel of audacious wit by the author of *I Shot The Hairdresser*. A narrative extravaganza in which characters appear and disappear without warning. Fiction has never been so strange. "Captivating, brilliant prose that may be blinding to the normal eye."—Kevin Sampsell
ISBN: 0-9639192-0-2 $6.95

THE ADVENTURES OF GESSO MARTIN by Karl Roeseler

A novel by the author of *Last Decade*. "Karl Roeseler takes a straightforward situation—a wandering rock star, a lion, seven French maids—and, with good humor and a charming light touch, rings magical changes on it. Particle by particle, with glittering clarity, the world of the fortunate Gesso Martin, the gentle chauffeur-cum-philosopher, gradually accumulates around us in an engagingly fantastic tale..."—Lydia Davis
ISBN: 0-9639192-1-0 $8.95

MONEY UNDER THE TABLE by Lewis Warsh

A collection of short stories by the author of *A Free Man*. "Lewis Warsh's stories are devastatingly good. Fragments of plain unlikely lives are enacted in expertly simple, sinuous prose. Characters evolve in a bewitching and scary realm somewhere between event and insight, at the unnerving center of what we take to be reality. These people are all too convincing—we wouldn't want to be them, but we probably are."—Harry Mathews
ISBN: 0-9639192-3-7 $10.00

DOOMSDAY BELLY by Susan Smith Nash.

A collection of short stories by the author of *Channel-Surfing the Apocalypse*. Susan Smith Nash possesses the rare ability to write about topical events and issues without being predictable or mundane. Oklahoma will never be the same. "These brilliant, often riveting apocalyptic narratives are so complex, edgy and darkly funny that it is almost a betrayal of them to point out the beauty of their style." —Jack Foley
ISBN 0-9639192-4-5 $12.00

HERE LIES

An anthology of short stories with the wicked premise that every story either features the telling of a lie or the presence of a liar. Stories by Etel Adnan, Charlotte Carter, Adrian Dannatt, Lydia Davis, Stephen Dixon, David Gilbert, James Kelman, A.L. Kennedy, Deborah Levy, David Lynn, Colum McCann, ZZ Packer, Karl Roeseler, George Saunders, Gilbert Sorrentino, Philip Terry, Lynne Tillman, Lewis Warsh, Mac Wellman, Dallas Wiebe and John Williams.
ISBN: 0-9639192-5-3 $13.00

Order from your favorite bookseller or directly from our distributor,

Small Press Distribution

www.spdbooks.org

800.869.7553 or 510.524.1668